The Stoneclad Chronicles

The Ember Within

Elisabeth B. Golson

ISBN 978-1-64300-919-3 (Paperback)
ISBN 978-1-64300-920-9 (Digital)

First Edition

Covenant Books, Inc.
11661 Hwy 707
Murrells Inlet, SC 29576
www.covenantbooks.com

Show me how to love in the darkest dark; there's only one way to mend a broken heart.

—"Beautiful Dawn," The Wailin' Jennys

TO MANY—MY PARENTS, WHO HAVE always been there to encourage, motivate, and teach; my husband, Tyler, who graciously listened to these thoughts before the ink hit the paper; Chattanooga coffeehouses for never kicking me out; and to my Father in heaven, who supplied every word you are about to read

CONTENTS

Prologue 9

Part 1: Merryn

Chapter 1: The Shadowed Mountains 15
Chapter 2: The Tribes of Tlogluck 19
Chapter 3: The Gathering Hall 27
Chapter 4: The Elites 33
Chapter 5: The Results 37

Part 2: Thaddeus

Chapter 6: The Dunes of Yehuda 49
Chapter 7: The Scavenger's Raid 53
Chapter 8: The Purest Heart 58
Chapter 9: The Charred Ones 63
Chapter 10: The Unanswered Truth 66

Part 3: Merryn

Chapter 11: The Ignition 75
Chapter 12: The Secret Prisoner 79
Chapter 13: The Awakened Answers 84
Chapter 14: The Tribunal 89
Chapter 15: The Surging Flame 96

Part 4: Thaddeus

Chapter 16: The Escape 105
Chapter 17: The Unexpected Guest 109

Chapter 18: The Ascent 112
Chapter 19: The Burning 117
Chapter 20: The Beautiful Mystery 121

Part 5: Merryn

Chapter 21: The Forest Escape 129
Chapter 22: The Surprise 134
Chapter 23: The Confession 137
Chapter 24: The Battle 141
Chapter 25: The Face 146

Part 6: Surge

Chapter 26: The Dark Prince 155
Chapter 27: The Bargain 159
Chapter 28: The New Legion 163
Chapter 29: The Meeting 168
Chapter 30: The Swallows 176

Epilogue 185
Appendix 193

PROLOGUE

THE HISTORY OF THE FOUR REALMS

(As recorded in the Book of Lore)

IN THE FIRST DAYS, THE Mover stirred together a dominion of man and spread them across the expanse of the earth. From the lush forests of the west to the great peaks of the east, we lived, as most do in the beginning, simple yet beautiful lives in man's vast home. Forged as through fire, Lasaria became the essence of perfection, a land unspoiled by faulty human arrogance and insatiable greed. We knew them not. As iron in the flame, we were refined and cleansed of any impurity, any darkness threatening our existence—our hearts the iron and the Stoneclad our flame.

The Stoneclad, a ubiquitous presence of hope and peace, became our light, the purpose behind our existence, and the only means to perfect harmony amid the Lasarian Lands. Fashioned from the bonds of brotherhood and tested through fire, the Stoneclad held the mystery that was our perfection—the truest expression of peace. To ensure the Stoneclad remained pure, the Mover chose a kingly line, four descendants of the lineage of Halvor, to be the exact expression of its light: endurance, love, strength, and wisdom.

Over time, Lasaria stretched beyond its first boundaries, and its people made for themselves four realms of power in response to each guardian's reparative gifts. For when the Stoneclad was formed, its guardians, having fulfilled their predestined purpose, forfeited their own powers to become spiritual expressions of light and goodness. This act marked the creation of the Stoneclad and became the source of our peace. And thus the four realms were born.

From the lofty peaks of the great Shadowed Mountains rushed the breath of an enduring pursuit of life. A reviving hope stretched across the realms, filling the people of the east with the desire to maintain peace. With this desire came a unique power, fitting for a life of constant pursuit. As Shadowmen, their ability to heal was rumored across the lands as an act of sorcery. They became ageless, as if frozen in time, and therefore, greatly respected by all.

Down the mountain's steep hills to the edge of its wide base lay the vast Desert of Yehuda. Its sands numbered as immeasurably as from a never-ending source and stirred wildly from the thoughts of the pure of heart. From the depths of his soul, a Yehuda's sight, unblemished and innocent, brought forth a gleaming future for the Lasarian Lands. For in their minds spun images of times forthcoming; and through enchanting voices and mystical art, they could see beyond even the brightest hope. Many traveled far across the realms to find their fortune in the eyes of a Yehuda.

West of the desert sands, running from the northern boundary to the southern coast, the crashing waves of the Sydan Sea echoed fiercely from the force of an unfailing strength. An obscure watery depth, filled with secrets and mysterious creatures, surrounded the Sydanese. They were as stars floating adrift the moonlit night, luminous and radiant in power. Both an incredible and terrifying gift, the remarkable strength of the Sydanese was both beautiful and dangerous to behold, for with much strength comes much power—one that can so easily ensnare and corrupt the strongest of brothers.

And finally far to the west of the Lasarian Lands, the winding paths of the mighty Vihaan Forests brought with them a discerning mind, able to guide men along a steady course. The minds of the Vihaanan were as the expansive sky, clear and open to all. No thought remained hidden but rang with resounding clarity throughout the forest realm. A Vihaanan's all-knowing gift secured the position as advisor to the Halvor line, but the ability to know as well as control the mind ensured that peace roamed freely throughout the realms.

And so with each realm sprang forth an ancient power from the Stoneclad guardians that spread a continuous light throughout the growing lands… so long as they kept it ablaze. But with any great gift comes the consequence of its abuse. Soon, darkness began to spread across the realms, a sickness that took root inside our hearts. Each realm's gift became a means to more power.

Men quickly began to lose themselves amongst the shifting sands of foreknowledge. As darkness spread in the heart, a Yehuda's gift of sight became scattered and disconnected. Pictures of perfect clarity soon depicted only the fragments of a once bright future, broken, until the images slowly faded to nothing. Their blindness then gave way to complete and utter darkness.

Like their desert brothers, silence soon befell the race of Vihaan. With each bend of the winding forest came the desire to control and manipulate the mind. Men sought to overpower the other through deceit and cunning. Soon, their discerning thoughts became piercing screams of confusion, followed by an inexpressible silence. With each growing urge of power, the darkness spread and gave rise to creatures of despair.

Once men but reborn from fire and char, these dark creatures fled also from the swift waters of Sydan. As with the flood of evil, their human strength began to intensify. It grew to unimaginable heights and carried a weight far more powerful than the most forceful current. But as their power grew, their mind fled and gave way to unspeakable madness. Now with strength incomparable to any man, the Sydanese sought absolute power and allowed no one to stand in their way. Forming an army of Charred Ones, they demolished village after village, adding more to their numbers daily as darkness consumed the realms.

As hope began to fade across the Lasarian Lands, the mystical healers of the Shadowed Mountains looked on in fear. Unable to reverse the effects of the Charred Ones, the Shadowmen fled deeper into the mountains, hoping to preserve what they could of the guardians' light. As time passed, the realms grew dark, and hope seemed lost. Hidden behind their fortified walls, the people of the Shadowed Mountains disappeared and faded into legend, while the life wind grew still behind the mountain peaks.

The Stoneclad was broken, scattered ruins of a once great land.

Darkness covered the hearts of many.

But buried deep within flashed a small light, an ember amongst the ash.

It waited silently, patiently, for its guardians to rise up once more.

Part 1

MERRYN

The Shadowed Mountains

THE MOUNTAIN AIR WAS COLD and had grown much colder in the last few days. The winter winds rushed forcefully throughout the thinning forest, as fresh snow veiled the small village as delicately now as the wildflowers in the spring. How she missed those tiny blossoms and the warmer weather that came with them. Somehow, the cold had a way of piercing down to the bone, awakening parts of us that were buried deep within. Merryn sat cross-legged at the furthest edge of the cliff, overlooking the village she called home.

From her vantage point, Tlogluck seemed minuscule compared to the mountains encasing it. Below, the luminous waters of the Crystal Lake appeared as a giant mirror, reflecting the storm clouds above. She dropped a stone the size of a small apple and watched as it made a slight ripple in the deep waters. From where she rested, Tlogluck was not a village lost in the stiff peaks of the Shadowed Mountains but a floating city whose resting place was the bright horizon. She felt a rush of wind against her delicate frame and longed for it to carry her over the lake and on to… anywhere.

A chill ran down the length of her back, causing Merryn to shiver as she wrapped her brown cloak tight around her neck, its fur warming her skin. To many, the Ridge was a place for young daredevils, a brief relief for those battling the emergence of adulthood. For others, it was considered a rite of passage, upon the completion of their apprenticeship, to dive off the edge into the lake below. Though she was considered one of the best and bravest of her year, Merryn had no intention of taking the leap, not today, anyway. For Merryn Swordwielder, the Ridge was nothing and everything at once. It was an escape, a time to breathe in the chilly mountain air and clear her mind of the noise encircling her.

Having just completed her eighth and final year of apprenticeship, her small frame and delicate features were in direct opposition to that of others in her tribe. She didn't have the look of a Swordwielder, nor had she the mind of one. A Swordwielder sought the limitless praise of others and possessed an innate capacity to protect the village—neither of which were characteristics she claimed herself. Instead, she felt a constant war raging inside. Her mind fought desperately to desire these things, yet her soul refused to accept them.

In their place lingered an overwhelming sense of dread at the inevitable completion of her apprenticeship and what the results would mean for her future. Her fear came not from becoming a Swordwielder; on the contrary, her skill and proficiency with a blade rivaled many men in her tribe. In fact, rumor had spread among her year that she would become the youngest tribune since Tlogluck's inception. No, she was quite capable of her calling, but completing her training would mean that she would never leave Tlogluck. She would stay and guard the village like all the wielders before her, and the dream that had remained in her mind for years would slowly fade into nothing. It was this reality that haunted her, sending chills up her spine, not the cold nor the faint voices of tribesmen in the distance finishing up a day's work.

As the sun eased its way down behind the western peak, she could almost hear Anata's voice calling for her. She would have to reemerge from her mountain of solitude and rejoin the life that never felt like her own. For a moment, a sudden impulse captured her attention, urging her to jump down into the icy transparency below and lose herself in the mirrored clouds, not to die but rather to preserve one final moment of freedom. Almost as soon as the idea crossed her mind, the voice rang out behind her with a resounding clarity. Soon, she thought, she would be back amongst the various tribes: Swordwielders falling in from the eastern ridge after scouting the village perimeter; or Lorefolk putting away freshly sharpened quills and scrolls worn heavily from practiced hands; or Euphony hauling into the Gathering Hall harps, flutes, and other instruments for the village's nightly enjoyment; or Earthbearers wholeheartedly preparing food for the night's feast.

Merryn watched as her guardian seemed to glide gracefully up the rock-laden path to the Ridge, wearing the usual grimace that told Merryn she was yet again in trouble. Anata was the only mother figure she had ever known; and she treated Merryn as her own child, making no distinction when faced with the many stares and whispers of nosy tribesmen.

Growing up, Merryn's pale skin and brown hair flowed in stark contrast to the bronzed features and ebony waves of the villagers, and her small stature became more prominent through the years compared to the towering frames of other children her age. When her distinctly different appearance became the focus of teasing from the other children, Anata never faltered in her response to them; she merely smiled and replied, "The Mover saw personally to it."

No one dared to cross Anata, mainly because being the wife of a tribune had its benefits. Not only was Anata's husband a member of the tribunal, the leaders of the four tribes; but Tarquin was the tribune of the Swordwielders, the protectors of Tlogluck, making him more like a king than a mere tribe leader. So often, Merryn was badgered for being Tribune Tarquin's favorite, insisting she had an unfair advantage.

What they didn't know was just how difficult it was being the daughter of Tarquin Swordwielder, how he incessantly pushed her to be the best. They didn't see those nights after everyone left the pitch where she remained behind to spar with the tribune himself or those mornings when everyone arrived at their perimeter post twenty minutes early, but because she'd already pulled a double the night before, she, consequently, arrived five minutes late. As a result, she would spend the cessation of the day digging scouting trenches along the ridgeline.

Such was the life of Merryn Swordwielder. An onlooker might say it was a good one, a great one even. But to Merryn, there seemed always to be something missing, a giant void that simply couldn't be filled in this small village, tucked beneath the snow clouds of the Shadowed Mountains. Something remained lurking inside her memory, eager to burst forth and take her far beyond the edge of this snow-clad ridge to an unimaginable future. For as long as she could remember, this void etched itself deeply in her heart, ever increasing, until she believed her very soul would become a hollow nothingness. But she had no way to fill it, no way to search for it; and worst of all, if she remained in Tlogluck, she might never have the chance.

The Tribes of Tlogluck

MERRYN TURNED TO FIND ANATA directly behind her, wearing that not-so-fond smirk of disapproval. "Could you not hear me calling for you? We'll be late to the feast."

Merryn thought for a moment. "The wind was really howling, 'Nata," which was more of a half-truth; and Anata knew it, raising her eyebrows. Merryn grinned. "I got lost in my thoughts is all," she said as she wiped the snow from her wool pants and brushed the mass of tangles from her face.

Anata sighed slightly. "Well, I knew you needed a moment or two's peace after the last few days, so I let you be." She then continued, gazing at Merryn sharply, "But you should've started down when you saw the sun setting. It's too cold to be out here past dusk. And I nor Tarquin have laid eyes on you all day."

"I know. I'm sorry," replied Merryn. She didn't like to make either of them worry, but she desperately needed the solitude. Sensing this need, Anata issued a light smile that warmed her entire face. The deep brown of her skin burnished brightly amidst the snow-white backdrop. She clasped her hand with Merryn's and gazed down into her daughter's deep blue eyes, until she returned the smile. They both turned to face the lake overlooking the village, looking like two complete strangers.

Merryn was short and muscular from years of hard wielder labor. Her hair, matted in mahogany brown knots from the gusts of mountain wind, fell in long strands along her face. When the sun shone upon her head, however, her hair turned a bright auburn, except for the one blonde streak that framed the rim of her face. As she stood, the brown woolen cloak she wore around her back dropped to her ankles, completely engulfing her petite body. Her boots, rising to her knees, masked her legs in a mound of ties and fur. She didn't consider herself beautiful, at least not like Anata, but she seemed to attract no fewer admirers across her tribe—though she knew this to be more an attraction of power rather than love. Being the tribune's adopted daughter came with its own set of interests, but the fact that she could beat any one of the boys in her year gave her more pleasure than courting one.

Anata leaned forward to pull the hood of Merryn's cloak over her head and smiled subtly. With her dark skin and jet-black hair pulled back into a tight bun behind her head, Anata had a tall and slender frame but carried herself in a way that gave off incredible strength and poise. Her features were worn and tired with age, but her eyes exuded a strange calm like the Crystal Lake before a summer storm. She wore a large coat of solid white fur, which fell to her waist, and highlighted her gray trousers and knee-high boots, trimmed with more white fur. No matter what she wore, it somehow seemed to enhance her beauty in a way Merryn could not explain, like she was destined for more than this tiny village. It was this feeling that drew her and Anata closer over the years. Merryn knew both Anata and Tarquin had left Tlogluck long ago before she was born, but neither would speak of it, especially to Merryn, as if they needed to shield her from the reason.

There was no doubt they loved her; they made every effort to ensure she had everything she needed and more—not in a material way but more out of necessity. It was as if she *had* to be the best. Everything she learned was carefully constructed and tested for accuracy like the village's survival rested on it. In the last years of her apprenticeship, however, Merryn couldn't shake the feeling that she was training to protect more than just the village—that her years of training were meant for more.

There on the Ridge, Anata standing closely beside her, Merryn pondered on her previous years in the small village, sheltered from the outside lands. She had spent her principles, the first five years of schooling, learning twice the amount of information as everyone else. As customary for children from the ages of three to seven, each morning was spent learning the basic fundamentals of each tribe; but when the afternoon came and all the other principles returned to help in their home tribe, Merryn was forced to recite the morning's lesson from memory until the information was engraved in her mind or until Anata was satisfied with the rhetoric.

Upon completion of their principles, children are chosen by the tribunal for their apprenticeship based on tribe proficiency and their natural inclination toward one of the four tribes: Euphony, the musically inclined; Earthbearers, those responsible for the production and harvest of crops; Lorefolk, the teachers and recorders of legend and history; and the Swordwielders, the guardians and protectors of the village. Here, apprentices remain for eight more years of intensive study until the tribunal considers them worthy for their position. Then they become an active member of Tlogluck. When Merryn turned eight and the time for apprenticeship arrived, it came as no shock to anyone that she was chosen as a Swordwielder.

It was these thoughts that paraded in her mind; and before she realized, the two of them were down the mountain and hadn't spoken since the Ridge. Each assumed the silence was for a different reason. Anata knew Merryn hated the cold and perhaps the lack of conversation might expedite the journey; but lately, she sensed that Merryn had more concerns than she confessed to her—the very concerns she herself felt.

It was true; the last few days of training had been extremely difficult for Merryn. With the conclusion of any eighth year, wielder apprentices had to complete what was known as the elites, which were a series of tests designed to ensure mastery of wielder knowledge. If they passed, they were assured a position in the ranks of their tribe; if they didn't, they were to repeat years seven and eight—which was beyond humiliating. Merryn knew of only one boy to fail the elites, Brannick, who was a few years older than she but was now finally in his eighth year, the same as Merryn.

But passing her elites occupied only a fragment of Merryn's mind. The rest was consumed with a longing deep within her gut to go to a place she knew not where. All she could do was hold on to the feeling; and despite her attempts to smother it, the urge grew stronger with every day like an inextinguishable flame. Yet as the days passed, it felt more like an ember that couldn't ignite; there was a spark but no kindling to feed the flame. It was a nightmare from which she never truly awoke.

There was also the unavoidable truth that the nightmare didn't frighten her but created an excitement like that of jumping from the Ridge for the first time. There was no fear, only the notion that what she was feeling was right. What she dreaded most was that the ones she loved might uncover the truth—that the nightmare was no nightmare at all, merely a dream after which she longed to chase.

As they rounded the curved road that led to the entrance of Tlogluck, Anata spoke the first word since their descent from the snowy peak: "Hungry?" she asked.

Merryn thought for a moment. "Not really," she replied as her stomach rumbled growls, quickly revealing her lie. She *was* hungry. She'd been on the Ridge nearly the whole day and hadn't eaten a bit since first feast that morning.

"I imagine Margo will have a roaring fire for us to warm by. You'll thaw out soon enough." Anata paused as she shifted the weight of her pack to her right side and rubbed the outside of her arms to warm them. "Are you nervous about your results? Tarquin said you performed beautifully. You've no need to be anxious."

"I'm not nervous—just tired, I think. Maybe the culmination of it all is finally setting in."

"Have you thought anymore about his offer?" she asked.

Merryn shrugged slightly and looked off toward the lake. She *had* thought about it. Becoming second under Tarquin would almost guarantee becoming tribune when she was older, a position of which any good apprentice dreamed. But the same lurking concerns from earlier filled her thoughts, and she picked up the pace to shake them from her mind. She *was* really hungry, but she especially didn't want to have this conversation again. Not now, not with Anata. Instead, she was reminded of her hunger by yet another ferocious growl.

As they passed the quaint dwellings of the villagers with their freshly thatched roofs and smoke billowing from each stack, she thought of the people who inhabited them. She imagined the Earthbearers exhausted from a day of busying themselves in the Gathering Hall. Merryn's mouth watered at the thought of roasted hare stew, filled with tender potatoes and plenty of vegetables from the stockroom. If there was anything about the mountainous winter she liked, it was the warm broth and abundance of vegetables that filled her plate most nights. She smiled at the image of Tribune Margo, who was as wide as she was long and with the temper of a lion, scurrying around the hall ensuring every man, woman, and child was pulling his weight. The women, adorned in stain-covered aprons from years of tedious cooking and cleaning, chopped mounds of vegetables and freshly stewed hare meat for the night's meal.

The Earthbearer children did their part by sweeping floors and collecting and washing dishes, being careful not to break a single one in fear of Tribune Margo's wrath. The men occupied their time arranging chairs and tables along the walls in the large open space of the Gathering Hall. The firewood, freshly split, lay in impressive heaps next to the Grand Hearth, a monstrous stone fireplace that scaled the height and width of nearly the entire side of the hall.

Once an Earthbearer in her year, a boy named Brogan wanted to see how many *new years* he could fit inside its mouth. Squeezing them in as tight as he could, he had nearly twenty pressed against the sides when Tribune Margo walked in. She had him cleaning the night's feast dishes for a month after that.

She thought of the Lorefolk as they rolled up mountains of scrolls and stacked the nearly empty inkwells in neat rows along the shelves of the Historia. Like most buildings devoted to apprentice training, the Historia was as enormous as the Gathering Hall; but instead of a grand fireplace, there stood countless rows of shelves filled with ancient books and rolls of parchment. Its interior would appear as a dungeon of dust and darkness if not for the hundreds of candles burning from the enormous waxed-covered chandeliers above. Merryn always thought it a bit foolish to have the history of the Shadowed Mountains resting in such an incendiary location, but no one else seemed concerned.

Along the far end of the Historia, opposite the large shelves, there were four large tables for the days' recitations from Tribune Casca, a scrawny and sinister-looking weasel whom Merryn always thought to be a colossal bore. Day after day, tribesmen alternated between recitations of the village legends and histories, mending worn books and scrolls, sharpening quills, and replenishing their village supply of ink. Though parts of Tlogluck's history were quite fascinating, Merryn never shared the same enthusiasm for the trade as other Lorefolk. After listening to incalculable complaints from a younger Merryn during her principle years, Anata had hoped she might in time appreciate the value in the trade but to no avail.

The only tribe other than Swordwielder by which Merryn seemed fascinated was that of the Euphony. According to the Lorefolk, the Euphony is the oldest of the tribes and supposedly became the founders of Tlogluck, though Merryn had her doubts. The legend speaks of an ancient language of song in whose speakers had magical powers of sight and accordingly *saw* the ultimate ruin of the realms and the unexplainable survival of their people. The vision led them to this very mountain valley next to a lake as clear as crystal; thus Tlogluck became a village, named after the first Euphony tribesman. As years passed and their village grew in number, the leaders decided they needed protection from the outside, records of their long history, and provisions to feed the growing village; and thus the other tribes were born.

As a result of the legend, the Euphony felt a sense of superiority over the village, which brought about much resentment from the other tribes. The feeling of supremacy slowly faded, however, when years led to decades and no one in the tribe *saw* anything other than what was right in front of them. Eventually, the Euphony became known only for their beautiful music and the even more beautiful Tribune Sophia.

Tall and willowy, Sophia was the youngest of the current tribunes and had the feisty energy to prove it. Her hair fell in sleek black curtains of silk below her waist, which greatly accentuated her striking appearance. Merryn still recalled the puddles of drool from the mouths of each of her male tribesmates during principles. Their infatuation was utterly ridiculous but caused a roar of laughter when they were called on to recite one of Tlogluck's arias.

Merryn had the voice of the Euphony but, to Tarquin's delight, felt the blade of a Swordwielder best suited her talents. When it came time for her apprenticeship, she was chosen as a Swordwielder and spent the rest of her time learning the art of battle.

As protectors of Tlogluck, Swordwielders led quite a different life than that of the other tribes. For one, they had no grand building in which to study. Instead, they had the pitch, a large field that covered acres of pastureland and was used for sparring matches, training in physical fitness, and learning the rules of war. Most days were spent either on the pitch or scouting out along the perimeters of Tlogluck. Evenings and nights were for guard duty, which apprentices couldn't do until fifth year and even then had to be accompanied by a head wielder.

But Merryn had been running guard duty with Anata and Tarquin since before she could remember. Her earliest memory was peering into the night's sky atop Tarquin's horse, Reinhold, listening to the tales of long-lost kingdoms and their noble kings and queens. She would drift to sleep with visions of far-off places and names of people she imagined she knew.

As this thought grazed her mind, her stomach gave a leap, perhaps from the hunger pangs, which were fiercely returning—perhaps not. Finally reaching the Gathering Hall and facing the enormous doors of the entryway, Merryn closed her eyes and anticipated the smell of sweet-smelling stew and the barreling laughter of her tribesmen.

For a moment, she hesitated and felt a tinge of guilt for her previous thoughts about leaving the village, her home. She loved its people and the memories she'd made with them, but the void was never filled by any of it—as much as she wanted it to be. Anata leaned into the doors and pushed them aside. They creaked heavily and swung open, revealing the merriment awaiting them. Merryn smiled; this was her favorite part of the day.

THE GATHERING HALL

IN ALL OTHER PARTS OF the day, every soul in Tlogluck worked in his tribe but not for the day's last meal. The night feast was the only time a villager was tribeless. As they entered into the great room, Merryn smiled at the familiar sight and breathed in the warm smells that encircled her. The whole village came alive with the joys of togetherness, despite their fatigue of a long day's labor.

The tribunal sat with their spouses around their distinctive square table on the far end of the hall. They smirked and spoke in tones that made themselves seem even more important while pretending to listen to each other's not-so-interesting conversations about that which no one cared. There, she saw Tribune Casca squinting his eyes and pursing his lips to make for the full effect of his prominence. Merryn gleamed at Tarquin, sitting passively yet never revealing his apathy toward the conversation. He caught her eyes across the room and wrinkled his nose as if it itched, though Merryn knew that was the sign for rescue. She smiled slightly and pushed forward.

As they moved across the hall in the direction of the tribunal, Anata wore her usual warmhearted smile and graciously spoke kind words to each tribesman as they walked along the rows of tables lining the way. Merryn trailed after with her hands clasped behind her back, giving the same gracious nod to the men and women whom she passed.

Everyone spent the last hours of the day at the night's feast. They roared with laughter over how so-and-so slipped during a sparring match and landed in Annabelle the cow's fresh patty. Others were reminiscing about the time such-and-such turned over a new bottle of ink onto Tribune Casca's oration on the Legend of the Shadowed Mountain Mammoth. They belly-laughed and joked of how they would've felt badly had they not heard it three times before.

The eighth-year boys and girls were brandishing their tribe pins, a symbol that meant they were at the end of their apprenticeship, while third- and fourth-year girls *oooohd* and *ahhhhd* over which boy they would soon begin courting. Merryn grimaced at the idea. The thought of marrying at all made her stomach churn, but marrying any of the boys in her year made her positively green with nausea.

She saw a group of wielders in the same year as she, sitting at a table nearest the front window to the right of the tribunal. Merryn gave a slight chuckle and shook her head. *Trying to hear the conversation, no doubt*, she thought. She waved as they beckoned her to sit with them. Nodding, she held up her hand to motion she would join them after speaking to Tarquin and the other tribunes. They smiled and returned to their *discussion* of the day's events.

Though night's feast was a time to unwind, there were always formalities that accompanied the gathering. Tarquin would stand and offer a blessing of the feast before Tribune Margo had the night's preparations placed along each table. Then everyone was quick to serve themselves hearty portions from the lavish spread. Once everyone seemed duly satisfied, Tribune Casca would present the night's itinerary.

On most nights, this meant recitations about news of the village, such as birth and death announcements or marriage declarations. This was followed by a lengthy oration on some historical finding, which was all too often the same one; and the night concluded with the reminder that the work of Lorefolk was a sacred thing and not to be ignored. The counsel was mostly aimed at children in their principles who spent their time napping or catapulting peas at Bigsby Earthbearer's enormously large belly. At the conclusion of his oration, Tribune Sophia would stand to signal the Euphony's closing song, indicating the end of the night's feast.

Tonight's agenda, however, would be rather different and especially exciting for those in Merryn's year, as they had just completed their elites the previous evening. Consequently, Merryn and her fellow tribesmen had the day to spend as they pleased, anxiously awaiting the announcement of their results that night. The majority of her fellow tribesmen spent the day in the village, parading about snobbishly like they owned the place. And because it was freezing outside and the waters of the Crystal Lake would be all but welcoming, other apprentices decided to find alternative means of exhilarating entertainment rather than take the perilous leap off the Ridge as was custom after elites. Also, given that all other tribes' *elites* were issued in the spring, summer, and fall months, they merely postponed the ritual for when the weather was quite a bit warmer. She, however, chose to spend her time in the mountains away from everyone else, trying everything in her power to *not* think of her results and what they would mean.

Making their way to the head table of the tribunal, Anata took her seat beside Tarquin, who issued her a pleasing smile and gently kissed her cheek. Merryn gave a dutiful nod to her adoptive father before turning her attentions to the rest of the Tribunal.

"Good evening, Tribune Margo. You've once again outdone yourself. It smells incredible in here, and I am famished," she said, patting her stomach.

Margo, a short lump of a lady, gave a gracious smile that illuminated her whole face. "Why, Merryn, you're always too kind," she replied as she gave a hearty chuckle.

Turning her attention to Casca, Merryn stated, "And to you, Tribune Casca. Good news of the village tonight, I hope?"

"Indeed, young Merryn. And I'm certain you're anxious to hear of your results, no doubt. Tarquin has spoken of nothing less," he said in his customary tone.

Merryn hesitated, looking rather uncomfortable, as Tribune Sophia stepped in to her rescue.

"News we shall hear of soon enough, Casca," she said, patting her fellow tribune on the hand. "I'm sure Merryn would like to find some sustenance. We all know what an anxious spirit can do to the stomach." With a reassuring smile toward Merryn, Tribune Sophia motioned for her to join her friends at the next table, whom Merryn noticed were staring wondrously at the discussion being held. As she met their gaze, they turned their heads suddenly back to their own table. Merryn smiled at her friends, knowing they'd be all ears when she approached.

"You're quite right, Sophia. Merryn, you must be hungry. I'll have Josephine bring you out a fresh bowl and some hot cake rolls," said Tribune Margo, turning to summon a girl not much younger than Merryn.

She nodded graciously to Tribune Margo, thanking her immensely for her thoughtfulness, said her pleasantries to Tarquin and Anata, and made way for the table of fellow eighth-year wielders, who were all too eager for her to be seated. Just as she took her seat next to them, a young bearer girl brought out another large bowl of hare stew and a plate full of steaming cake rolls for the table to enjoy. Merryn closed her eyes and sighed in relief as she savored the very moment she had been imagining for an hour now. She then fell into discussing the day's escapades from each young wielder's day of freedom.

As she slurped her first bowl of stew, relishing each delicious spoonful, Aiden, a burly boy with short, dark ringlets, piped up and asked what everyone else wanted to know, "Sooooo, what was that about?"

"Oh, they just wanted to know how it felt being the new wielder second," she lied. Everyone knew Aiden was not so secretly gunning for the position, and she relished the thought of making him flush with anger.

He grimaced and gave a taunting *hehehe* as the others nearly spit cake rolls across the table. The girl next to her, Cadence, a former Euphony tribesman, nudged her playfully. "No, seriously, did they mention anything about our results? I've been sick to my stomach all day. I couldn't even think to help my mom organize the night's sheet music in the gallery."

Connor, a freckled-faced skinhead boy from across the table, leaned in with the retort, "Cady, you've been nervous since that first sparring session. It's a wonder you made it through elites," to which she responded with a roll, flying straight for his face. He caught it in his mouth and grinned brightly; Cadence blushed bright red. Every wielder in their year knew these two had a thing for each other since fourth year. Now, with the stress of elites behind them, the table's light and easy moods allowed for excessive flirtation. This discussion encapsulated everyone except Brannick, who sat quietly at the end of the long table. His ever-present scowl seared fiercely upon the laughing party. Merryn knew it must have been difficult for him to make friends with apprentices several years younger than he, but it wasn't from their lack of trying.

She recalled a time during the beginning of training last year when two boys asked for Brannick to show them the best way to hold the blade while leaping across long distances, a skill at which Brannick was especially good. He responded by grabbing both boys by the neck and dashing them to the ground on their backs. Needless to say, they figured out a method on their own. No one else cared to make much of a conversation with him afterward. Though something about his face produced a strange calm in Merryn, one she couldn't explain, and she was therefore no more intimidated by the boy than Tarquin.

And there he sat at the end of their table with his black hair, falling to his shoulders in curling ringlets, wearing the usual all black garb that made Merryn think he was in more of a grieving period rather than rejoicing over the end of his second set of wielder elites. Though, she guessed if anyone else she knew had failed elites and had to watch those in the same year advance into village society, they'd probably cover their face with ash and tear their clothes. So maybe his coping methods weren't that bad after all.

Just as these thoughts crossed her mind, Brannick looked up from the table to catch her staring at him. Merryn's eyes bore the look of embarrassment and surprise as she quickly turned to face the other apprentices and pray he hadn't noticed her staring.

Just then, she noticed a hush upon the hall as Tribune Casca ascended the stairs to address the room with his usual announcements. He then shifted to a brief explanation of tonight's significance and proceeded to explain the history of each tribe's elites. Merryn looked at her empty bowl and decidedly reached for the large pot of stew to ladle for herself another heaping bowl full as her wieldermates sat in eager anticipation.

THE ELITES

EACH TRIBE HAD THEIR OWN form of elites during eighth year, but tonight was reserved specifically for the Swordwielders. When the time approached, the head of the appropriate tribe would stand and motion for all eighth-year apprentices to stand in line in front of the tribunal table. He or she would then provide a brief description of each part of the elites and announce the top three ranking apprentices in each category; these would be the top contenders for second-in-command. Each tribe's categories varied slightly; but all reflected some form of strength, innovation, and natural inclination for the trade.

For Earthbearers, this meant something along the lines of how quickly one could split a heap of firewood and fill the Grand Hearth, whether one could create an original meal from random ingredients and keep Tribune Margo from spewing it all over the place, and finally whether one could manage the productivity of a personal garden. These gardens covered the left end of the pitch and, more times than Merryn cared to count, had a sparring wielder trampled upon the sprouts in a bearer garden. Thankfully, Tarquin had a fence built to act as a barrier between the two fields. Merryn was often envious of the peaceful diligence with which they worked. Then again, she didn't think the life of apron wearing or wood splitting would offer the same excitement that she needed in the long run.

For Lorefolk, the strength bit seemed the most excruciating of all elites, as it was more strength of mind than body. For three days, apprentices had to endure daily orations from Tribune Casca and answer questions from the information accurately in front of a panel. Next, they were to provide an original conclusion to a village legend, which more times than not had Tribune Casca roaring with obnoxious laughter, claiming they were too ridiculous to be recorded. Finally, their tests ended with a recitation of an excerpt from the account of the *History of the Four Realms*, completely from memory. Merryn had a fine memory, Anata frequently saw to this fact over the years; but the idea of sitting under the utterings of Casca for eight more years made Merryn swoon with dread, taking a pass on this tribe.

The Euphony elites were the only ones in which members from other tribes could view. Other than their introduction of an original piece and their ability to conduct other members of the tribe in a cantata, the Euphony's final test was as beautiful a sight to behold as it was tragic. Merryn could recall the looks of pure exhaustion on the faces of young apprentices after playing their instruments or singing their songs for hours at a time. This test was meant to prepare them for or at least remind them of the long hours of battle. Though they never fought in hand-to-hand combat, it was the job of the Euphony to sing or play the songs of victory over the warring tribe during conflict, as a symbol of their endurance and power. Had she not been chosen as a wielder, Merryn thought for sure she would have been in the Euphony. Tribune Sophia frequently praised her musical talents, especially that of her voice, during her principles; and something inside Merryn always tugged at the idea of a power brought on by music, even if it was merely a legend. Still, Merryn knew this was not the tribe in which she belonged.

The Swordwielder elites were, perhaps, the most physically trying of all tribes, and rightly so, given that all wielders were Tlogluck's first and final line of defense against invaders. It was not that the villagers were not welcoming by nature; in fact, Tlogluck's people had a history of traveling to various villages across the realms. It was only after the fall of the four realms that Tlogluck became shut off from the world and a self-sustaining village. Merryn had never actually seen an invader, but Tarquin was always quick to remind her that the lack of sight didn't mean they weren't there. Wielders were prepared either way.

During their elites, apprentices were first to compete in sparring matches. Each time, an apprentice would stand in the middle of the pitch with a blindfold across his or her face. Then at Tribune Tarquin's mark, other apprentices would advance toward the middle and attack. This test required the use of all senses but sight and lasted until only the one in the middle remained. This often ended badly for everyone without the blindfold.

The second test was Merryn's favorite, as it was more a game of endurance and ingenuity than test of swordsmanship. In this task, apprentices had one hour to hide themselves somewhere in the mountains. They left during the night, and the *game* lasted until either all apprentices gave in from the cold and returned home or were found by Tarquin or another apprentice, in which case each one had to surrender. The last apprentice left was declared the victor. Being that Merryn was extremely gifted in the art of stealth and actually preferred solitude to group activities, she faced neither the problem of being found nor giving in from the cold, for she loathed the idea of returning to the pitch more than she did the icy wind.

The last task, however, was not Merryn's strong point, as her size proved somewhat problematic. The race marked the conclusion of the Swordwielder elites but still had its share of difficulties. Beginning at dawn, apprentices set out to make for the summit of the Shadowed Mountains. The race was not as much about speed on foot as it was about strength of mind and body; apprentices had to climb the peak to reach the summit. Not surprisingly, the first to reach the top won the race. Though Merryn was a fair climber, her small size played a disadvantage compared to the reach and strength of wielder boys in her year. Fortunately, making it to the top at all was as good as getting there first, in Tarquin's opinion.

Anyone who completed each task to Tarquin's satisfaction fulfilled the apprenticeship requirements and was elevated to Swordwielder. It was then they dropped the name of their family and wore the name of their tribe.

As Merryn slurped her third bowl of stew and wiped her mouth on her sleeve, she saw Tribune Casca descend the stand and realized she hadn't paid attention to most of it. Though, he was sure to throw in his usual reminder of Lorefolk significance before inviting Tarquin to announce the results for which everyone was most eager. He ascended the steps to the stand and gave Casca a genuine smile of gratitude before extending both arms in front of him, revealing the dark ink embedded along his forearms. He stood, a colossal mass of strength and intellect, towering over the members of each tribe. He, like Anata, had the same dark skin and black hair, though his was graying more with age and years of deeply rooted hardships. The room fell to an utter silence as his deep, raspy voice thundered throughout the Gathering Hall. "Eighth-year apprentices, please take your place before the tribes."

The Results

MERRYN FELT HER HEART LEAP into her throat as Tarquin called for the wielder apprentices to make their way to the front of the hall. She, along with her other tribesmates, rose from the table and began to file in line, one after the other. Aiden led the way, closely followed by each of the young wielders. Merryn fell in behind Cadence and noticed as she stole a quick grin at Connor, who brought up the rear. Her year held the largest number of wielder apprentices in two decades, twelve total, and with nearly as many girls as there were boys.

Marco, Remi, Matthew, and Gwendolyn came from bearer families. While Cadence, Zuri, and Kristoff were from the Euphony. Connor and Helena were the only Lorefolk—which left Merryn, Aiden, and Brannick as the only natural-born wielders. Though, Merryn wasn't technically natural-born, a fact of which Aiden frequently reminded her, Anata was always quick to reassure her that natural ability exceeded natural birth every time.

During principles, children would spend their mornings under the instruction of each tribune; then they would spend their afternoons attending to the necessary needs of their home tribe. Though parents secretly hoped their children would apprentice in the tribe of their birth, no one ever protested if they were chosen for another, which was often. Wielders were the only tribe where numbers truly mattered, as they needed to train more members in order to offer sufficient protection of the village. However, over the years, the number of apprentices gradually decreased in each year, which many attributed to the lack of invaders in the Shadowed Mountains; though Tarquin always said it was the result of the villagers' own cowardice. It was therefore a great shock to everyone when so many apprentices were chosen as Swordwielders in Merryn's year.

As the line of apprentices approached their mark, Tarquin briefly reiterated parts of the wielder history, which Casca emphasized earlier, making him nod emphatically in approval. Tarquin then began to explain in greater detail the proceedings of the wielder elites that had transpired earlier that week.

*****

The pitch was still white from the early morning frost and crunched underneath the boots of wielder apprentices, as they made their way to the middle of the field. The icy wind blew all around, piercing their cheeks with needlelike sensations. Merryn shook the cold from her mind and fought the urge to retreat to the warm covers of her bed, which would have been a severe disadvantage. Today marked the beginning of her elites.

She looked around at the faces of the other apprentices, eleven other boys and girls in her year, who had endured much of the same training as she throughout the eight years of their apprenticeship. With such clarity could she recall their initiation ceremony—the look of nausea on the tiny young faces as they marched to the pedestal and awaited the decision of the tribunal. She could feel the mixture of emotion from each apprentice who jumped tribes, their parents nodding with reverential approval. The cheers from fellow tribesmen as they gained a new member exploded throughout the Gathering Hall.

Merryn remembered the nervous jitters as they gathered together on their first day of official training as Swordwielder apprentices. And now here they were on the last days of their training. The boys stood stoically, trying to hide their anxiety behind looks of strength and indifference—all except Brannick who appeared more annoyed than anything. The girls displayed the quiet calm that was attributed to most wielder women. Merryn stood in the middle of the pitch displaying signs of neither hidden anxiety nor overconfidence; instead she looked to the eastern ridge, praying for signs of the rising sun so her face would thaw and regain feeling in her fingers and toes. But they were awake long before the sun; a long day of sparring sessions awaited them.

Soon Tarquin appeared in front of them; in his hand was the blindfold that would force their inner senses to awaken, as they defended themselves against the onslaught of young assailants. Wielders were to be prepared for all possible forms of attack, even in the darkest of places where sight was impossible. She should have been nervous, she thought. But perhaps the years of over preparation on Tarquin and Anata's part forced a sense of peace and acceptance with her fate; perhaps it was the feeling of misplacement that seemed to engulf her thoughts over the last months. Either way, Merryn did not appear to wear the same look as of that worn by her fellow apprentices.

Because their years of training had prepared them for what they were to expect, the need for further instruction was not necessary. Instead, Tarquin merely smiled and, with one fluid motion, tossed the blindfold high into the air. A freezing blast soon caught hold and carried it straight for its first participant; the other victims as they were later called—for it never ended well for them—scattered and awaited the call from their Master Tribune.

Upon seeing the blindfold land in Brannick's large hands, Merryn took off, sprinting for the southern tree line. Brannick wrapped the covering tightly across his eyes and grasped his blade with a firm but relaxed grip. Everyone else resumed his scouting positions. Viewing a seemingly empty field, Tarquin gave a solemn nod of the head.

There was a brief pause while a single dove flew from one of the trees opposite Merryn. Brannick made no motion but stood as calmly as if he had just awoken from the most pleasant of dreams.

Suddenly, a figure moved in from behind where the boy, clad in all black, stood in the middle of the pitch. It was Aiden, moving stealthily toward Brannick.

No shock there, thought Merryn in her position along the southern perimeter. She slowed her breathing and awaited the attack. As Aiden drew nearer to his destination, Brannick did not so much as shift his footing, and Merryn thought for a moment that perhaps he would be overtaken. Almost as soon as the thought crossed her mind, Aiden raised his dulled blade to tap the top of Brannick's head and begin the sparring with the element of surprise. No sooner had he gone in for the attack than Brannick spun to his side, ramming the hilt of his sword into Aiden's gut, dropping him to his knees. Merryn gave a slight laugh as the other apprentices filed in. Some teamed up to provide misdirection; others fell in individually, waiting for their moment to attack. One after one, Brannick dodged blows, dealt his own, spinning and twisting in fluid motions, appearing as the natural-born wielder he was. She wondered how he could have ever failed his first round of elites, but the thought quickly left her as she saw her moment arise. She stole a look at Tarquin, who narrowed his eyes; she knew what she had to do.

Moving closer but making not a sound, she saw Marco on the ground yards in front of her. As he stood up, preparing to go in for another attempt, she followed in closely behind without his knowing. Brannick was occupied, fending off a combination of blows from Kristoff and Zuri, as Marco stepped in. Merryn ducked down, awaiting her moment as Brannick and Zuri's blades clanged together, making a circling motion around their bodies before her blade fell from her hands. He then issued a front kick to Kristoff, knocking him backward and immediately lifting his arm, clotheslining Marco to the ground. He wrapped his hands around his throat and doubled over, and Merryn saw her mark.

With a fluttering motion, she bounded forward and leapt off Marco's back toward her target, thrusting Marco's face toward the pitch, still damp with frost. *I'll apologize later*, she thought briefly. With her blade in hand, she flipped over Brannick's head and landed opposite his position, intending to issue the final blow. Just as she neared the side of his neck, he turned and knocked her blade away from his body. They fought for several moments as their swords clashed and clanged, ringing like bells across the pitch. Once again, Merryn thought she had him beaten when he swiftly responded with another crashing blow, gliding effortlessly around her. Merryn's head spun briefly as she looked up and saw no one. Almost as quickly, she turned to see Brannick's large fist crashing into her face. Everything went dark.

This was why they assigned the entire day to sparring matches. Most apprentices needed time to regain consciousness. Merryn awoke to Brannick's face looking down over her; he was smiling. Her vision blurred slightly as she considered his features. She had never once seen him smile. His dark eyes held neither a trace of pity nor shame but rather unadulterated wit. He was *laughing* at her. Brannick leaned his arm down to help her up, and Merryn winced with pain. She wiped her nose on her sleeve, which was then covered in blood. She recoiled slightly at the sight.

"What did you do that for?" she yelled at Brannick.

"I didn't know it was *you*," he said defensively. "Honestly, I hoped it was Aiden." As he said this, he glanced over to his right, where Aiden lay strewn out across the grass. He still had not awoken.

Merryn took a moment to laugh at this image of Aiden, whose mouth lay open with a trickle of drool flowing out one side. "Well, that was a cheap shot," she said forcefully. "You could have broken my nose!"

Brannick shrugged his shoulders apathetically. "Ah, you heal fast," he stated plainly. "Anyways, you disarmed me. The goal *is* to defend yourself. I merely reacted. Besides, you'll have time for retribution." As he said this, he tossed the blindfold in Merryn's direction and took off behind her. She smiled wryly and placed the cloth, now damp with perspiration, around her eyes.

My turn, she thought.

As the sun made its way down the western horizon, the pitch was literally crawling with young apprentices, who were weary from the day's sparring. Tarquin gathered them all together and congratulated them on a job well done. They were one day into their elites and felt as if they'd been at it for weeks. One good thing about wielder elites, however, was the abundant food that awaited them in the Gathering Hall. Margo always had a special feast for apprentices during their elites where they could eat until their hearts' desire, though Merryn's desire was first and foremost a piping hot bath.

And so the week progressed as the elites continued. The following day was, in Merryn's opinion, entirely more fun than the sparring sessions, as all she had to do was avoid being caught by another tribesman. She was especially good at this and had no trouble spending the day strolling through the forest. One might find this the less logical means of keeping hidden; but for Merryn, her small size made this quite plausible, as she was not sauntering along the base of the trees. No, Merryn Swordwielder was high atop the lofty branches, bounding from tree to tree. Of course, had it been the spring or summer months, cover from the foliage would have been preferred, but she made do with the camouflage of her brown coat and the incredible breadth of the trees in the forest. There she remained until she heard the screech of Tarquin's pet falcon, Gawain, signaling the conclusion of the task and that she had indeed won.

The final task was the climbing race to the summit. As with every other task, the apprentices awoke long before sunrise and made their way to the pitch, anticipating Tarquin's call to commence the final task of their elites. As he gave the signal, the apprentices took off on foot for the base of the mountain, but the race had just begun. Upon reaching the foothills, the apprentices had to endure miles and miles of climbing to reach the summit.

Merryn thought back to her days of training under Tarquin when she was still in her principles. They would fill their packs with food and spend days hiking and climbing along the peak. This was her favorite memory as a child and how she loved to think of Tarquin, not as a tribune but as her father. It was here she first peered over the treacherous edge of the Ridge and conquered her fear of heights. She and Tarquin sat for hours just talking, discussing each other's hopes and dreams and often avoiding the ever-penetrating question of why she looked so differently than everyone else in the village. She knew she had not been born in Tlogluck—that Anata had found her as an infant and brought her back to her village. But beyond that, she knew nothing else. And perhaps Anata and Tarquin thought their love for her would overshadow her longing to know her past, but it never would.

Merryn recalled these thoughts throughout her ascent up the mountain. The rocks were slick with ice, and the piercing wind further numbed her fingers. There were several instances in which she thought she'd have to descend and begin a different route; but glancing about eagerly, she'd find just the hold to press upward and continue the climb. Her breathing was slow and deep, and other than the chill of the wind, it was the only thing she heard. Climbing had a way of overshadowing things; and the increasing altitude was just what she needed at this moment. She didn't want to think of Tarquin or Anata, of her elites, of becoming second. Right now, she just wanted to climb and breath; because right now, that's what life was. It was what was needed to fight this particular battle; and as she reached the final ledge to the summit, she pulled herself up just enough to see Aiden grasping the red flag. But she didn't care; she had made it to the top. This battle was won, and that meant her *elites* were over.

*****

It was aspects of these days that Tarquin recounted to the tribes in the Gathering Hall. He elaborated on the skills and techniques necessary for each apprentice to complete the tasks at hand, focusing specifically on the strengths and weaknesses of each apprentice. This was how they were sorted, based on their abilities. Finally, he came to the conclusion of the evening's agenda where the top three apprentices were named and regarded for the position of second-in-command.

Days before, Tarquin had asked Merryn what she thought about the position if it were offered to her. She gave him no absolute answer, assuring him that she would think on it. For any wielder apprentice, the answer should have been obvious, but Merryn was certain she wanted neither the responsibility of becoming second nor the possibility of her dream of leaving the village of Tlogluck to close in around her. But most of all, she feared the disappointment in Tarquin's eyes when she refused him.

As Tarquin prepared to recognize the top three apprentices, the crowd grew even more silent as anticipation soared throughout the room. Merryn could almost feel Aiden's boots shuffle, preparing to take his position on the stand. She and Cadence shared a smirking glance, and both rolled their eyes, grimacing at the thought of taking orders from Aiden. Tarquin paused, then began to speak earnestly, his deep voice slicing through the tension in the large room, like a wielder blade gliding through the air.

"As you all know, not only do the elites signify the termination of the apprenticeship, but they also determine the Swordwielder's second-in-command for the forthcoming year, a valued position among the tribe. This young man or woman will ensure that the daily responsibilities of a wielder are administered effectively and to the benefit of the village as a whole as well as assisting in the training and overseeing of wielder apprentices. This also means that in the event that I, as tribune of the Swordwielders, am unable to fulfill my duties, he or she, as second-in-command, can and will protect the village until another tribune is named in my place."

Tarquin paused, allowing the responsibilities of this position to sink in deeply with the apprentices standing before him.

He then began, "Brannick, stand before your tribe."

At these words, a gasp was heard throughout the hall as Brannick Swordwielder made his way up the platform. Merryn knew that to offer the position of second to a repeater was not merely rare but never done; however, something in the way Brannick carried himself gave him the appearance of a tribune. She believed the rest of the tribes must have seen it too, as they all fell silent with awe. As he stood beside her adoptive father, standing nearly as tall, something in Merryn's stomach leaped.

"Do you, young Swordwielder, understand the responsibilities set before you?"

Tarquin spoke the common phrase as Brannick respectfully responded with, "I do, Master Tribune, and accept them wholeheartedly." They bowed to one another, and Brannick took a step back on the platform.

Again, Tarquin prepared to speak another name. Merryn held her breath.

"Aiden, stand before your tribe."

A roar of cheers erupted from the hall of tribesmen. Aiden gleamed and traversed toward the platform but not before eyeing Merryn with his usual annoying glare. She simply stared back, praying he would trip and fall.

Upon reaching the top of the platform, Aiden turned to face the crowd, trying to appear as tall as Brannick but with no success. Tarquin once again asked the other apprentice, "Do you, young Swordwielder, understand the responsibilities set before you?"

Aiden maintained his smug demeanor and replied, "I do... Master Tribune... and accept them... wholeheartedly," bowing his head and pausing dramatically for effect throughout the declaration. Again, the crowd sent waves of applause toward the platform.

Finally, tension built as Tarquin prepared to name the third and final apprentice. Merryn felt Cadence squeeze her hand, and she felt bile rise up in her throat. She was now regretting the amount of hare stew she'd consumed. A drop of perspiration fell from the top of her head and down the left side of her face.

Just as Tarquin opened his mouth to speak what Merryn feared was her name, the giant doors of the Gathering Hall burst open. The entire hall turned to see Rawlins, a wielder scout, surge through the entrance, wearing the expression of one who'd just seen a ghost.

"Invaders!" he shouted, "along the western perimeter!"

The entire hall of tribesmen turned to stare at Tarquin, who simply narrowed his eyes and said with such calm, "All Euphony, Lorefolk, and Bearer tribesmen, return to your homes. Swordwielder scouts, assemble on the pitch."

Merryn was just about to turn and fall out when he added, "All except principles and apprentices, you will return to your homes. Anata will see to it you make it there safely."

Merryn glared at Tarquin, wearing the same perplexed look on her face as the other eighth years. As if sensing their frustration, he said, "You have endured three long days of hardship, and if indeed you are needed, I will call for you. But for now, you must rest. Go, all of you."

And that was it. Perhaps the Mover heard her plea for deliverance from what she knew Tarquin was about to announce; perhaps, Tarquin doubted her abilities. Whatever the cause, Merryn was sent straight to bed. No protest was sufficient enough to ward off Anata's piercing threats if she were to sneak out. Disbelieving what had just transpired, she fell to her bed, thankful to be there after the last week and yet frustrated with Tarquin's command. *Hadn't this been what they'd trained for? Why now were they again treated as children?* Merryn had just the mind to storm back into the den of the dwelling she had shared with Tarquin and Anata since before she could remember when sleep suddenly poured over her body and swallowed her mind.

*****

Darkness filled the room except for the glimmering light of a candle resting atop a stone hearth. A woman lay trembling amongst a heap of blankets. She was crying and holding her swollen belly that had, only moments ago, held a child. Before her, on the opposite end of the room, stood three young children, and behind them were two hooded figures. To the right of the woman stood another cloaked figure, this one clutching a small bundle in its arms. Their hoods and the darkness of the room hid their faces.

Suddenly, the woman on the bed gasped and cried, "No. Wait. Leave her be."

The hooded figure turned to face her, then leaned forward, placing the swaddled bundle in her arms, a baby.

The woman, frail and dying, smiled and uttered in short raspy breaths, "She will need what memories she has. For she alone can help them to remember whom they are…"

The vision trailed off, and Merryn awoke with a jerk. Fragments of this same dream had haunted her for years; only this time, Merryn knew the dream was no dream at all, but a distant memory. For the first time, Merryn felt she knew the strange woman on the bed. This time, she knew the woman was no stranger; she was her mother.

Part 2

THADDEUS

THE DUNES OF YEHUDA

HIS EYES JOLTED OPEN. A hazy light poured in between the slats of wood covering his window. His sketchbook laid strewn open upon the floor where mounds of sand rested in scattered heaps and piled itself into each corner of the small dingy room. *Must have dozed off*, he thought. He hadn't slept in several nights; and even when he had, it was never very long. Sleep was a rare find for Thaddeus, as the life of a scavenger meant long days and even longer nights. When the clan wasn't running raids in the cover of darkness, they were sorting through scavenged junk, most of it useless, or parading through villages, selling what they could. They ate when they had food and slept when they weren't busy running from the people they'd just scavenged. Such was the life he had known for nearly eight years.

Thaddeus leaned down to retrieve his sketchbook, dusting off the collected sand. He carefully flipped through the pages to even out the corners where they had bent from the fall. The drawing he'd been working on the night before—a girl, with deep and distant eyes, who had occupied his dreams for years—stared back at him. Her face, tired yet determined, somehow gave him strength. He found himself wishing he would dream about her whenever he could sleep, not in a romantic sense but more out of curiosity. He felt as if he needed to know her and would awaken disappointed because he didn't. Still, he drew her; he had memorized her features. Her eyes seemed to stare straight through him. Her beauty was subtle yet enchanting, as if she had a secret that only she knew. He remembered the first time he had seen her; he had been much younger, only a small child, but could recall fragments. It had been the most terrifying day of his life, one that had changed how he lived to this day. It was the night he lost his father.

Thaddeus stared blankly as the memory coursed through his mind.

The screams were all around him, piercing through him in concentrated surges down to his very bones. Memories came back to him in bursts of smoke and haze. *There was the fire, and his father, covered by more screams. People were running everywhere, and he was scared—so scared. Don't lose heart,* he heard his father repeating over and over again. *Stay pure,* he thought. *Stay pure… and you're safe.*

Thaddeus shook the memory from his head at the sound of heavy footsteps nearing the doorway of his tiny quarters. *Bexler,* he said to himself as he stood, shaking the sand from his clothes. His bed, a heap of dusty rags and animal hide, cracked under his weight. He doubted how much longer the old thing would last. He approached his door just as Bexler banged heavily with his fat fists.

Swinging it open at the sound of the first bang, Thaddeus stared inches away from the man under whose keeping he had been since he was nine.

"Bex! I was just coming to find you!" he said with a smirk that stretched across his face. He continued, "How was your night? Pleasant, I hope."

Bexler made a gurgling sound from his throat and arched over to spit a disgusting mass inside the doorway, just missing Thaddeus's foot.

Lovely, thought Thaddeus.

"Boy, I've a mind ta whip ya good and hard till yer legs bleed."

Thaddeus gulped as he stared firmly back at Bexler, whose breath reeked of some vile liquid as he continued, "It's near nightfall, and I've got a full wagon outside..." He paused and squinted his eyes. "Now tell yer Bex this, how's are we supposed ta eat tonight if we ain't got nothin' ta trade? Hmmm?"

Thaddeus glared back at him, then, rolling his eyes, turned to throw on a sandy-brown cloak over his tunic. "I'm coming. We returned so early this morning, and everyone went straight to the Tav. So I..."

Bexler cut him off, abruptly saying, "So ya thought since nobody stayed behind ta help that ya could just run and grab some shut-eye, that right?"

Thaddeus pushed past him through the sand-filled corridor that separated the bunks of each scavenger. He was lucky to have had his own room for as long as he did; the man who had shared with him before had been caught during a raid. That was three weeks ago, and no one had seen him since.

Bexler yelled after him, "Well, I ain't haven' it. If we ain't got an empty wagon, we ain't got no room for more jewels. No jewels, no food. No food, *noooo sleeeeep*!" Screaming the last part across the hall, he ruined any chance of sleep for anyone else.

Good, thought Thaddeus. Then maybe he would get some help unloading Bexler's wagon full of jewels. *Jewels*, the term seemed abysmally illogical. He had not pulled one piece of anything worthwhile from that run-down piece of garbage in years. Though when one relies on junk for food, any scrap could begin to seem like a diamond in the rough, and this place was indeed rough.

As he pulled back the curtains of the makeshift door to their barracks, the sun's rays fell onto his face, illuminating the day's final moments of light and heat. The dunes could be strangely beautiful—if one were merely passing through and had no reason to stay longer than a few hours. Any longer than that and he'd realize how dreadfully wrong he'd been. Looks can most assuredly deceive the eyes, and the sands of Yehuda weren't the best place to be deceived. The days were bitterly hot, with threats of the Swallows at every step forward and the quick hands of other scavengers leering from behind. The nights carried the same fearsome threats but with a mixture of stinging ice and sand in the winds that made one long for the heat of the day.

He paused for a moment, soaking in the last bits of heat. The sun began to sink behind the mountains, turning the dunes into a blisteringly cold wasteland, and Thaddeus shivered in preparation of the night's scavenge. He saw Bexler's heap right where they'd left it in the early hours of that very morning. Thankfully, everything appeared untouched. He saw the same bits of tin scrap lying across the length of the wagon. Underneath it, the shards of glass jutting out from one side scraped against the only valuable pieces they'd found that night, a worn-out wooden rocker and one wooden chest, with one hinge hanging off the corner that made the lid sink inward.

Thaddeus made his way over and began, piece by piece, unloading and organizing what he thought they'd be able to sell. The bits of stale bread and broth the tin and glass would buy made his stomach ache with desire, but he knew the wooden pieces were truly treasures in comparison, allotting for at least five or six meat rations. At least that might aid Bexler in forgetting that he'd chosen not to unload the wagon sooner.

After he'd hauled off the last of the jewels, he ensured they were locked in Bexler's stall and ready for trade the following day. The wind began to pick up—and with it the sand, flowing in frequent bursts, stinging his skin. He grabbed the hood of his cloak, wrapping it around his head and face in the typical scavenger fashion, and made his way across the camp to the edge of the dunes. He sat atop the nearest ridge, his back against the vast Yehuda Desert with the Shadowed Mountains, deep and distant, in the horizon.

THE SCAVENGER'S RAID

NIGHT AND DAY WERE FLIPPED for scavengers. Thaddeus spent his days sorting and selling Bexler's prized merchandise, and on the rare-occasion eating and the even-rarer-occasion sleeping. For a while, the difficulty of the life proved overpowering and often resulted in his falling asleep during a raid and ended with a number of lashes from Bexler's whip. Soon, however, he grew accustomed to the change or rather less accustomed to the lashes. This night, Thaddeus sat on the back of the rickety wagon with several other men in Bexler's crew as they made their way down the winding desert path.

Netheq, who had been with Bexler the longest, since before Thaddeus had arrived, sat atop a pile of dirty blankets, allowing him to see out over where Bexler rested atop the bench, steering Al Haml, the camel they'd collected months ago. He was as grimy as Bexler but half his size; he was bald with no hair on his face either. Instead of eyebrows, Netheq had intricately drawn tattoos tracing all around his face, giving him wild animal-like features. He turned his head to look toward Thaddeus and smiled; his teeth, blackened and rotting, were sharpened on the tips, only adding to his fascinating appearance. Thaddeus was at first repulsed by the strange man but, over the years, seemed to develop more of a fondness to him than any of the others in the clan. Netheq was by no means compassionate, but his unrestrained humor toward the other members often balanced out Bexler's brash conduct.

Sitting directly to the right of Thaddeus was Wormer, a newer implant in the clan, but no less disgusting, who reeked with an odor of curry and fish. He was always sucking up to Bexler, annoyingly copying his motions and mimicking his behavior. Being around Bexler himself was nauseating enough, but Thaddeus cringed at the idea of having *two* Bexlers. More often than not, he found himself wishing Bex would get annoyed and eventually put an end to Wormer's antics.

Behind them were the twins, Mierisch and Hanoch. They were perhaps the most intriguing of the crew with their identical foreign appearance and strange staring habit. More than once, Thaddeus would glance up to find two sets of almond-shaped eyes peering eerily in his direction. Thankfully, it was a custom they frequented on everyone and not merely Thaddeus himself. After a while, he dismissed it as merely a foreign way of getting to know others. They rarely ever spoke more than a word; but when they did, it was always uttered from the both of them simultaneously, making them even stranger to behold. Even Bexler himself seemed to be taken aback by them, which was perhaps the very reason he kept them around.

That seemed to be Bexler's way of *collecting* members for his clan; one needed a talent, which he deemed useful. Netheq's catlike behavior offered undeniable craftiness, a necessary skill for scavenging in places they weren't welcome—which was everywhere—and for making a quick getaway—which was always.

Wormer's scavenging wasn't of much use, as his stench could be detected a mile off; but he came with Al Haml, who was useful. The trader who sold him to Bex said they couldn't be separated, so he took them both. Fortunately, Wormer could manage to make something edible from whatever they could afford that week and so granted him the title of hash slinger of the clan.

Thaddeus, however, could neither sneak nor cook but seemed to possess a unique set of qualities that Bexler deemed more valuable than gold. Thaddeus was undeniably gifted in the powers of persuasion and could talk even the filthiest of traders into buying the most menial of items. His natural proclivity in drawing images of the items' usefulness greatly aided in these transactions more than once. He sat back in the wagon and thought about the night he first put his skills to the test.

He had been only nine years old and had been rummaging through a pile of scraps when Bexler came across him during a night raid of their own. Thaddeus remembered leaning down into a large can, attempting to reach for some sort of scraps to eat, when, upon pulling himself back up, he looked directly into the eyes of a wild cat. This was his first encounter with Netheq, who then proceeded to grab the entire can, along with Thaddeus, and carry it back to Bexler. Young Thaddeus, covered in grime from head to toe, stood too afraid to scream and simply glared back at the two men. Netheq, looking more muddled than anything, tossed the can into their wagon and whispered something to Bexler. He then cast a devilish grin down onto the boy, realizing the value of Netheq's recent discovery.

Soon they hauled their scavenged goods off toward the next village with young Thaddeus in tow. When the sun rose the following morning, he was in an entirely new village surrounded by mounds of sand and dust-covered huts. It was here that Bexler had the mind to sell him for profit. And upon realizing his fate, Thaddeus knew he had to do something.

"What'll ya give me for the lad?" Bexler's scruffy voice came barreling into the trader's tent.

Several ruddy-looking men peered through the entrance and glared at the boy, looking extremely confused but fascinated. One of them, their leader, Thaddeus assumed, edged closer to where he stood under the weight of Bexler's fat arms and spoke in a menacing tone. "Where'd you find this one?"

Pulling Thaddeus back, Bexler answered threateningly, "What's it ta you? I found him, and I'm willin' ta sell. Ya want him, or don't ya?"

"Aye, 'old on. I was just askin'. Don't be so quick to bounce there, Bex. How much you want for 'im?"

Bexler thought for a moment and eyed hungrily at a hanging hog leg. It had been a while since they had any meat and never had they had any as fine as what was hanging nearby.

Thaddeus glanced around him, noticing the men and women standing around the tents. There were no children, a notion that further threw him into a panic. His brow began to moisten with perspiration as his shoulders sank underneath the weight of his impending future. He looked back at the cart on which he was brought and observed the various pieces of junk that filled its interior. Several large pieces of metal, some rope, glass bottles of various sizes, three or four wads of cloth, and the very can, which led him to this fate, lay packed into the cart. He noticed a small piece of paper on the edge of a table inside the tent, used for recording transactions no doubt, and an idea suddenly coursed through his head.

He spoke hesitantly in a voice no louder than the soft wind that blew through the morning air. "Umm… excuse me, but could I perhaps make you a better offer?"

Bexler jerked, suddenly taken off guard by the boy's words. "Why ya littl'… ," but the man inside the tent cut him off.

"Quiet! What did ya have in mind, boy?" he said, a slight grin spreading across his face as he turned from Bexler to Thaddeus.

Thaddeus looked up at Bexler, then at the trader, breathed deeply, and said, "Could I borrow that paper and a bit of lead? I want to draw you something."

"Draw something?" Bexler shouted. "We ain't got no time fer ya tricksy games, boy. Now shut ya trap!" He started to pull him away but was again halted by the trader's firm words.

"I said stop!" the man gleamed at Bexler, then turned to grab the paper. He pulled out a piece of lead point from his robe and handed it to Thaddeus with an inquisitive smile and continued saying, "If ya wantin' anything from me today, you'll not move that boy until he's showed us what he wants to show us."

Bexler grunted and reluctantly released his hold on Thaddeus. Nearby, Netheq glided over watching intently at the events unfolding.

Thaddeus took the paper and lead from the man and sat down to draw, glancing up every so often at Bexler's cart full of junk and the man's threadbare tent. The hoard of scavengers and traders sat enthralled at Thaddeus while he worked. After a few minutes had past, he stood up and handed the paper back to the man in the tent.

"What's this?" he asked, a bewildering gaze pouring over his face.

Bexler and Netheq both exchanged puzzling glances and leaned over to look at the drawing. A mixture of confusion and anxiety filled their faces.

Thaddeus looked at the men and answered, his voice appearing more confident than before, "It's your tent, or at least what it *could* be with the contents of his cart." As he said this, he raised his arm and pointed a finger in the direction of Bexler's pile of junk. On the backside of what held recent trading transactions now appeared an intricately sketched building constructed from the heap of rubbish Bexler meant to sell. "If you let me go, you can have all of this, and I'll even help you build it."

"Oy, and what do I get with all *my* jewels, boy?" uttered Bexler, appearing more intrigued than before.

"You get that ham you've been eyeing and that larger wagon over there." He looked to the trader, pleadingly.

The man thought for a moment and raised his eyebrows. "I'll not give ya my wagon, but the meat you can have as well as a few biscuit loaves. Sounds like a fair trade, Bexler? Whatta ya' say?"

Bexler looked to Netheq, who was staring confusedly at Thaddeus, then said, "On second thought, you take the fill of the cart but the boy's mine. We'll take the meat and be on our way."

From that moment on, Thaddeus had a front-row seat to every trade and often left with more food rations than Bexler would have ever dreamed. The wagon came on the very next trade and now, nearly ten years later, bounced them roughly as they made their way across the dunes to another raid.

The Purest Heart

THAT NIGHT'S RAID CONSISTED OF pillaging the remains of a village several miles west of the clan's camp. There was one main path that led through the village and on to the mouth of a small estuary. The pathway was lined with what appeared to be the remains of smaller buildings, probably the villagers' homes or shops, but now were no more than piles of ash.

As they scavenged through remnants of broken pots and pieces of charred wood, searching for anything they could turn into profit, Thaddeus made his way north of the village to the only standing structure, appearing somewhat intact. The roof drooped inward, its thatching vanished after years of disrepair. The wooden siding, rotting and caving in, leaned slightly to the left, barely keeping the structure from collapsing. A small porch wrapped the front of the dwelling under whose floorboards, splintered into large slats, revealed the soft ground below.

Thaddeus stopped abruptly upon seeing a small structure to the right of the building, closest to the creek. It was a small boat, mostly buried under years of earth and rotten from the elements. Suddenly, a wave of emotion washed over him, and he dropped to his knees. He was home.

*****

Shamra woke him early that morning; they were to paddle out onto the creek before the sunrise to practice his drawing. The scent of sizzling bacon and fresh eggs met him as he sleepily pulled himself upward off the soft goose feather mattress. His knees ached slightly from the previous day's assisting in the village market, a task in which Shamra frequently insisted they participate.

Most mornings, they would pack up a few drawings, mostly Shamra's, and make for town where they would sell for themselves what they could but help in the other booths when necessary. As a result, most of the day was spent hauling around cases of fruits and vegetables or kneeling on rafters, thatching the villager's roofs.

"Service makes the heart strong," Shamra would often recite. Even if that meant they worked all day in the other tents and sold nothing of their own, Shamra never faltered, maintaining his original notion.

"The Mover will always provide to those with a willing spirit," he would say. And sure enough, each time they were needed elsewhere, they never returned home without an abundance of food for the two of them to eat on for days.

Because of those days, however, it was necessary for them to wake early in order to have time to sketch and talk, just the two of them. It was this one such occasion for which Shamra stood over their tiny hearth with a plateful of fresh eggs and bacon for young Thaddeus, who clumsily strode over to his chair at the table. He plopped himself down with a thud as Shamra placed the plate before him.

Smiling, he said, "Sleep well, my boy?" He gave the bacon a flip on the skillet before serving a decent-sized helping onto his plate.

"Yes, sir, thank you," Thaddeus replied, wiping the sleep from his eyes. He placed one elbow upon the table and lazily propped his face against it, yawning heavily.

"Eat up. It's going to be a beautiful morning," he said excitingly as he sat in the chair opposite Thaddeus.

Thaddeus stared wondrously at his father from across the table. Shamra wore a full brown beard that covered the lower half of his face. His eyes were a bright green, much like Thaddeus's, and disappeared almost completely when he smiled. He wasn't a very large man but had a slender build, with tight muscles that had developed over years in the village. What Thaddeus considered most, however, was the look of his face; his features were hard, almost carved in stone, but relayed the kindest of emotions. His heart was always open, and from it exuded the deepest kind of love for all people, especially for Thaddeus.

Shamra raised his head and matched Thaddeus's eyes. He smiled, fondly saying, "Do you know what today is?"

Thaddeus looked at him quizzically and furrowed his brow. "Ummmm, I think it's fourth day. Am I right?" pausing to think. He then continued stating, "Yes, it must be, because yesterday was the market, and the market is third day."

Shamra couldn't withhold his laughter and chuckled gleefully. "Yes, it's fourth day, but it is also your birthday! Did you forget?"

Thaddeus gleamed at Shamra and leaned over his plate, laughing as he said, "Of course I didn't forget! I was only testing you to see if *you* had! I'm rather impressed, old man!"

It was true; Shamra had aged significantly over the years; the gray in his beard made that evident. Still, he prided himself on celebrating Thaddeus's birth. It was this reason they were setting out on the creek to draw, specifically so Thaddeus could capture the sunrise using the gift, hidden under the table, Shamra had purchased the day before.

"Ahhh, I see. Keeping me young, no doubt. Bravo," exclaimed Shamra, reaching down underneath the table to grab a rectangular-shaped package. He handed it to Thaddeus, saying, "I thought you might be able to use this on the water this morning."

Thaddeus reached for the delicately wrapped bundle, carefully removing the wrappings and tossing them to the side. In his hands, he now held the most beautiful leather-bound sketchbook, his name etched in gold script at the bottom. He glared at it with such awe and flipped through the pages to smell the crisp new parchment. He regarded Shamra lovingly as he exclaimed, "Papa! How did you…? It must have cost you… at least three paintings! Why did you…?" But he could hardly finish a thought, before Shamra was by his side, with his arms holding him in a warm embrace.

"Coin is but a trifle to the love that fills my soul for you, Thaddeus. Always remember that. If you have love, nothing else will matter. Nothing else." After he said this, he stood and beckoned for Thaddeus to finish his breakfast, saying, "Now eat."

Afterward, they paddled out in the small fishing boat onto the creek beside their home. It was there they spent the morning fishing and laughing over the events of the marketplace, awaiting the sun to rise.

Thaddeus recalled the time they were mending Mr. LaRoque's roof when Shamra drove the thatching hammer directly onto his hand. The two of them roared with laughter as Thaddeus mimicked the howling noise Shamra made as he bounded off the roof and into a fresh pile of straw.

Then Shamra reminded Thaddeus of the time Mrs. Barley's daughter Gretalyn planted a kiss onto his cheek for rescuing her cat, Nimbles, from a branch. Thaddeus's cheeks went red as the cherry pie she brought to them later for his "dashing chivalry," as Shamra put it. Thankfully, the sun began to shoot up from behind the trees before he could submit Thaddeus to any more embarrassment.

They spent the morning drawing the sunrise. It was indeed a beauty to behold. Shamra instructed Thaddeus on how to correctly hold the lead point and how to position the strokes so as to successfully capture the image. Once Thaddeus made his final stroke, he held the drawing in front of him and studied it critically.

Pursing his lips, he asked, "What do you think? Think it would sell at market?"

Shamra took it gently from his hands and frowned. After a moment, he said, "Oh no, Thad. We'll not be selling this."

"I know… I have more work to do. But it's a good start," he replied, a little disappointed.

Smiling warmly at the frowning boy, Shamra replied firmly, "I'd not sell this for the world, dear boy. It's worth too much." A sincere yet troubling expression darkened his face.

Thaddeus looked to Shamra, then back at his drawing. "What do you mean? It's not *that* good," he said, taking the picture from him.

"Oh, but that's where you're wrong, Thaddeus. On the contrary, it's very good," he said, looking straight at Thaddeus. "It's not the strokes of the point that make its value. It's the pureness of heart that brings it to the surface," he added, pointing a finger at his chest. "Aye, that's as valuable as gold."

Thaddeus leaned into his father's chest and hugged him tightly. Soon, the voices of village folk, rising for the day's tasks, were heard in the distance.

"Let us go then?" asked Shamra, reluctantly releasing his grip.

"Aye," replied Thaddeus. "To serve." They each grabbed an ore and paddled back in the direction of the voices.

The little boat glided smoothly along the murky creek waters as the day marked its new beginning. It was the best and worst day of his life. It was his ninth birthday.

THE CHARRED ONES

SHE LEANED HER HEAD TOWARD him and smiled ever so subtly. Her brown hair fell in long waves down her face. As she stared into his eyes, he felt an uncontrollable sense of sadness, like something was lost from him—something he couldn't get back.

This was the first time he saw her—the girl he would see for years to come but had never actually met. Suddenly, the smell of smoke filled his nostrils as he opened his eyes and slowly sat up in his bed. A bloodcurdling scream rang out in the distance toward the village. The next thing he knew, Shamra came bounding into his room.

"Get up, Thaddeus. Come here to me. Hurry!" he cried. Grabbing Thaddeus by the arm, he pulled him to the far corner of his room and pushed away a small wardrobe. Below it rested a tattered rug, and pushing it to the side, he revealed a small door cut away in the floorboards. He lifted it up with his fingertips and motioned for Thaddeus to come closer. As he lowered Thaddeus below, they heard more screams from outside their home. These sounded different from the one that alarmed Thaddeus only moments ago. They were deeper and appeared to be coming closer. Then the most horrid smell penetrated their senses—the smell of burning flesh—and engulfed his tiny bedroom.

Thaddeus peered up at his father, expecting him to barrel down the trapdoor next to him. Instead, he merely gazed down at him with the look of a broken heart and quickly tossed a wrapped bundle down beside him.

"Listen to me, Thaddeus. I want you to follow this passage out from under the house and run into the woods. Do you understand me?"

He didn't. "Papa, what do you mean? What's happening?"

"There will be a time for answers, my boy, but today is not that day. I need you to listen to me very carefully. Can you do that?" his eyes looked pleadingly down at Thaddeus, who nodded and began to cry. "You are special, dear boy… more special than you know. And not just to me but also to a generation of people—people who need you to remain true. So above all keep your heart pure, Thaddeus. It is the only way to defeat them. And remember to love, keeping your heart open always."

They heard a loud banging coming from the door of their dwelling, and Shamra yelled, "Go. Now. And do not be seen." Lifting off the silver torc surrounding his neck, he kissed it and threw it down toward Thaddeus. He then shut the door after him, covering it with the rug and repositioning the wardrobe over its original place.

Thaddeus sat in the dark with his knees to his chest, crying silent tears for his father. He felt the smooth metal of Shamra's necklace in his hands as he placed it around his neck, letting it hang loosely on his skin. He began to smell the smoke intermingling with the same putrid scent from before. His body shivered as he heard the sounds from above. A rumble of footsteps bounded into the room directly overhead, and he could hear muffled voices as they questioned Shamra. He heard a loud crashing noise and then Shamra's voice as he screamed in staggered breaths, "Don't lose heart… Stay pure." Another thud echoed through the house, this time sending chills up his spine. Then he heard the sound of rubbing metal, as of a sword from its sheath. Shamra repeated the phrase, this time with more difficulty, "Stay… pure… and you're safe." The next noise was that of a brisk swishing, followed by a loud thud as something large fell to the floor.

Thaddeus need not see to know what had just transpired. Grasping the metal between his fingers, he shuffled quickly underneath the house. He reached the edge and found himself facing the forest, nearly fifty yards from the entrance. Before he took off, he peered around the edge of the house, and a sight that haunted him for years later glared back at him. Flames and billowing smoke poured from the tops of the villagers' houses. The streets were crawling with men, women, and children as well as dark creatures he had never before seen.

Their skin was as black as tar and bubbled up on the surface; every inch of them appeared to be charred and was, no doubt, the source of the stench. Suddenly, one turned to face Thaddeus and yelled something in his direction. At once, one of them stepped from the porch of Thaddeus's house and turned to face him directly. Here, Thaddeus saw their eyes—large, white orbs that appeared to be glazed over with a sort of oozing film. The creature pummeled toward him, as Thaddeus fell backward. Peering down over him, the creature gave a slight smirk and leaned down. The smell was almost too much to bear, making Thaddeus gag as it stood inches from his face.

At first, he thought it might smash its charred foot down, and that'd be the end; instead, it merely gazed into Thaddeus's eyes, as if peering into his very soul. All at once, Thaddeus felt his skin begin to burn. Suddenly, the creature gave a rattled yelp, covering his eyes with his hands. It tumbled backward before tripping over a stump in the ground. As it fell downward, it simultaneously burst into a pile of ash.

Thaddeus stared, his eyes struck with surprise and terror. He quickly glanced around to see if anyone had seen what had just happened. No one.

Hastily, he stood and sprinted for the forest, stopping only once there to turn and see his village, burning under stiff peaks of flames.

The Unanswered Truth

FOR A LONG TIME IT seemed, Thaddeus sat at the edge of the nearly dried creek and wept. Though Bexler's clansmen weren't the brightest of oafs, they figured enough to leave him be for another moment or two, revealing more compassion at that moment than they had since they'd met.

It had been nearly ten years since he had been back to his home, the village of Danwebe, where he had lived for as long as he could remember with his father, Shamra. *Papa*, he thought. For years, his memories would rush with blurred images of that night but never as full pictures. Perhaps he had not allowed himself to visualize them with such clarity in fear of the pain the memories carried with them—in fear of this very moment.

He stood staring at the broken little boat, half-buried in sand, and felt shame for the first time in years. He had not listened to Shamra's words. He had not kept his heart pure. He'd helped others; he had been all but a slave to Bexler all these years, but it was never a service from his heart. That aspect he'd kept sealed, unable to truly love.

He turned his gaze and let it fall on the ruins of what was once the cottage he'd shared with Shamra. Of all the homes they'd destroyed that night, he'd wondered why his was left somewhat standing. Then he remembered the charred creatures, the ones with the white eyes. He remembered how it had stared down onto him—almost *through* him. But mostly, he remembered how it *felt*, the burning he'd felt on his skin before the creature staggered backward and erupted in ash. Thaddeus put his hand to his throat, feeling his pulse in increasing bursts, as a sudden thought jolted through his mind. *The torc*, he thought. Unwrapping the sash from around his neck, Thaddeus felt the cool metal, now tarnished with age, which hugged his skin much tighter than before. He pondered intensely as he stroked the ends of the strange piece of jewelry with his thumb and forefinger.

The body itself was nothing special—a thick silver strand that wrapped around his neck; but before connecting, each end stopped to form a sphere with a strange engraving in the middle. A smooth curved line lay horizontally atop each end with a smaller line crossing over it at its center. Thaddeus often found himself thumbing it over with his fingers as he drifted to sleep when he was younger.

Keeping the trinket concealed from Bexler all these years was no small task. Thaddeus was careful to keep it securely hidden underneath his clothes and out of sight. As a result, he rarely thought much more about it. The memories it brought forth came with more pain than fondness. But now, here he stood, ten years later, in the very place his father had last worn it.

Collecting his thoughts, he rose from his knees and turned in the direction of the cottage, rewrapping the fabric around his neck. Behind him stood Netheq, and if not for the ink on his face giving him a constant grimace, he might have appeared to be concerned. Thaddeus gave him a quick nod and continued toward the old cottage. As he neared the front entrance, he could almost see the events of that night unfolding before him—heavy charred footsteps bounding up the old wooden steps, creaking beneath the weight. The door—bashed in from the fearsome fists—now lay open and decaying upon the floor. Thaddeus carefully stepped inside the old structure and examined the room. Most of the contents were missing, either from decay or pillage. The floorboards squeaked underneath his weight, and he feared they might collapse at any given moment.

He passed an empty room that once belonged to him. The missing thatch on the roof allowed the moonlight to beam in faintly over the spot where his bed once lay. To the left, he saw the trapdoor that had kept him hidden from the creatures. Thaddeus winced at the notion of what had occurred in that room and turned to leave when another thought captured him—a faint memory. Shamra had tossed something else down there with him just before he'd slammed it shut. *I wonder*, he thought.

Crossing the floor to where the trapdoor lay, he bent down to lift it upward with his fingertips. Peering down, he noticed a pale light coming from other places along the cottage where the floorboards were either missing or damaged. He lowered himself down and waited for his eyes to adjust to the darkness. There wasn't much light, but the glow from across the house allowed enough for him to feel his way around the bottom. Sure enough, a little ways from the entrance of the trapdoor lay a tan-colored packaged, concealed by years of dirt and debris. Brushing off some of the remains, Thaddeus pulled the bundle from the ground and made his way back to the opening.

He placed the package on the floor above him, then lifted himself up to the tiny room. When he reached the surface, the package was no longer on the floor but resting in Bexler's fat, grimy hands.

"And what's this ya have here, ya blubbery littl' weasel?" he said with a threatening grimace.

Thaddeus sprung out of the opening and threw himself at Bexler but was caught on both arms by Mierisch and Hanoch. "That's *mine*! Give it back, Bex. Please," he responded pleadingly.

"*Puuhhlleeaase? Puuhhlleeaase*? Hear that, lads? He said *puuhhlleeaase*!" Bexler spit out mocking chants as he looked around the room at the rest of the clan. The twins looked to each other and returned a subtle smirk. Wormer stood behind Bexler to the right and laughed idiotically, while Netheq hunched nearer the doorway, showing no natural emotion, just the usual grimace from his tattoos.

Thaddeus kicked and jerked to free himself but to no avail. Bexler moved in closer, his breath rank with the typical draft of booze and filth. He was no longer laughing as he stood inches away.

"And tell yer Bex why I should just let ya have this bit of jewel? Hmmm?"

Thaddeus thought for a moment. "Because it has my name on it," he snapped.

The clan looked around confusingly; then Bexler let out an obnoxious laugh, shaking his enormous belly viciously.

"It does, do it? Well, let's just see then!" Saying this, he ferociously untied the wrappings and tossed them aside, revealing the nearly perfect leather-bound book underneath—the name *Thaddeus*, glowing in gold writing at the bottom. The others leaned in intriguingly; Bexler's eyes grew angry.

"Well, *so what* if it does! Don't mean ya keepin' it. We could have ourselves a right fine feast tonight for this littl' beaut!"

Truthfully, Thaddeus had only half believed what he had said to Bexler; but judging by its size and weight, he assumed Shamra wouldn't have intended for him to leave it behind. Yet he had; and by the Mover's grace, it had been safe from the wrong hands—until now, that is.

"Bexler, give it back. I mean it! It's all I have!" he yelled across the room.

Rolling his eyes and gargling a disgusting mass in his throat, he nodded at the twins and turned for the door. Before he could pass through, however, Netheq blocked his path and glared down into his eyes. He nearly disappeared from behind Bexler and would have completely if not for his being a few inches taller. Thaddeus stood, his eyes wide with shock.

The two men gazed at one another for what seemed like a lifetime before Netheq spoke, his words gliding off his tongue like silk. "I think you should give him his book back."

Bexler stared motionless, but his scowl remained.

Netheq continued, his smooth voice sending an odd chill through the air, "He'll have his book back now. And you won't lay another hand on him." As he said this, Mierisch and Hanoch released their grip on Thaddeus and stepped backward. Netheq gently eased the book from Bexler's grasp.

Another breathless moment passed. Bexler narrowed his eyes, leaning toward Netheq's face, and raised his pudgy finger at him. "That'll be the last time ya use yer fairy mind ruse on me, ya hear? Next time, I'll send ya right back where I found ya." He stole a quick glance at the book in Netheq's hands and then arched his neck, spitting a brownish liquid right atop Netheq's foot. The two men again exchanged glances before Netheq moved aside, allowing the big, fat heap of a man to pass. Wormer trailed close behind, followed by the twins, each glancing curiously at the man covered in tattoos.

Thaddeus had rarely heard Netheq speak but never had he heard anything like *that*. It was as if his very words chilled the air, forcing whomever he chose to do his bidding. Perhaps it was this talent that Bexler desired. For the first time since he had known Netheq, he found himself wondering about his past, where he had come from, where he had been, or whom he had been. Before he could think much more, Netheq trampled toward him, wearing what he knew to be a look of undeniable anger. He thrust the book hard into Thaddeus's chest and narrowed his eyes. He said nothing but simply swirled around and jumped through the whole in the ceiling, above where once laid Thaddeus's bed.

Breathing deeply, he looked at the carefully bound book in his hands. The golden script shone as bright as the day he received it. He lifted it to his nose and breathed in its scent, hoping to find some trace of the new leather smell. The smell of dirt and mold covered most of it, but he thought he could make out a hint of the familiar aroma.

Holding the back with one hand, he ran another across the front of the book before flipping it open to the first page. He found himself face-to-face with the first and only picture he'd drawn on its pages—the landscape of the sunrise from the creek. It was the one he'd drawn while on the boat with Shamra on the morning of his ninth birthday. The lines looked as fresh as if he'd just made them.

Thaddeus choked back tears as he flipped to another page. To his surprise, the page was covered in words of a delicate script. The handwriting was undeniable; it was Shamra's. Thaddeus glanced around to see if his friends had changed their minds, but they hadn't.

He was alone. He sat down atop the creaking floor and propped himself up against the wall as he read the final words from his father.

My dear Thaddeus,

I am writing to you on the night of your ninth birthday; and as I hear you sleep soundly, I pray to the Mover that you would cease to bear this burden and rather live out your days in peace. But because I know this cannot be, I fear I must write these words to you now—the very words I have feared since you were three years old. I was entrusted with them the very night I was entrusted with you. No, Thaddeus, I am not your natural father, though I have felt the love a father has for a son from the moment I carried you home to Danwebe, the village of my birth. Please understand that it was not my choice to keep this hidden from you. There were so many times I wanted to tell you, but my duty as your protector held me back. I tell you now only because I fear what would happen if I were to wait any longer.

Something is coming, Thaddeus, something from which I have kept you hidden these last six years. I write to you now as I prepare my heart to be severed from you indefinitely. But I plead with you, my boy—do not lose heart. Do not fear their evil, as does the rest of the world. Remember my words, and keep your heart pure, Thaddeus. I hear them coming. Soon you will rise, and I must leave you with these words and book alone. But I trust the Mover will see you to safety until we shall once again meet. There is so much more to be said, but I am afraid you will have to learn it on your own. Let your heart guide you, and it will lead you to th—

The last words were scrawled upon the page as if written and cut off in great haste, and Thaddeus knew the reason. Tears rolled from his face and stained the parchment. The words were still stinging in his heart.

Shamra had not been his father.

But as much as the truth of those words pierced his soul, there was a part of him that knew it to be true. They looked nothing alike, other than the same green eyes. He never spoke of his mother—where they had met, what she had looked like, when they had Thaddeus—only that she had died. A part of him was almost relieved to have some answers, even if it wasn't the whole truth.

His mind whirled on the way back to the campsite, as he tried to ignore the biting tensions that filled the wagon. Netheq trailed behind them on foot instead of his usual perch at the front. Thaddeus wondered if it was by choice or punishment. Before long, he caught himself drifting in and out of sleep, visions of his past shaking him to consciousness. He could not sleep, would not sleep—not now, not with so many unanswered questions.

The sun was just beginning to make its way over the horizon, as they pulled into the scavenger campsite. But there was something strange about the bustle of commotion in the small village for so early in the morning. As soon as they came to a stop, a stocky bearded man approached the wagon, speaking in short, winded breaths.

"You might want to get back on that thing, Bex."

Bexler glared at him as if the man's words were the dumbest thing he'd heard and replied, "And why would I want ta do that, Bobble?"

The man named Bobble returned a look of surprise before he stated hesitantly, "Because they're comin' back."

"Who is?" growled Bexler.

"The Charred Ones."

Part 3

MERRYN

THE IGNITION

THE SOUND OF TARQUIN'S DEEP voice stirred Merryn back to reality. The dream that had just occupied her thoughts scattered into the familiar images of haze and obscurity. She had this dream consistently since she was in her principles, always the same one; but never had it appeared with such clarity, both in picture and in understanding.

As she sat up in her bed, her head began to ache viciously. How could such clarity suddenly transform into utter confusion? Placing her head between her knees, she slowly began to rock back and forth as the questions began to flood her mind.

How could she possibly have visions of her mother? Who were those people dressed in black cloaks? Why were they being taken away?

Again, Tarquin's voice rang clearly amongst the crackling of a fire. *Anata had not gone to sleep*, thought Merryn. How could she, with news of invaders? Feeling a bit guilty for falling asleep herself, she soundlessly stood from her bed and glided across her room to the doorway. Carefully pulling back the woven tapestry that covered the entrance to her bedroom, she leaned her head to the side and listened.

Tarquin stood, dark amongst the shadows, with his back toward her. One hand was placed firmly atop the wooden mantle, another curled gently beside his mouth, a gesture he made often when lost in thought. Had she been able to see his eyes, she would have noticed they were ablaze with anxiety.

Anata sat on the hearth, her head tilted upward lovingly toward her husband. She was not wearing her usual calm demeanor but rather held a burdensome gaze, as if she knew something terrible and feared to speak it. Finally, the silence was broken as Tarquin once again began to speak.

"They've never ventured up this far, Anata. Something is driving them," he said, placing his hand beside the other on the mantle.

"How long?" she asked earnestly.

"There's no way to tell. With these numbers, it could be weeks—days, maybe."

"We must tell her, Tarquin. Now, before it's too late," she replied, placing her hand upon his large arm, covered in dark symbols.

He replied stoically, "She's not ready. She's still a child."

Merryn listened intently from across the room. She felt her face mold into a grimace at the mention of *child*.

Anata furrowed her brow and stood next to her husband, a look of firm but tender love in her eyes. "What's your true concern, dear—that *she* is not ready or that *you* are not ready to tell her?"

He turned his eyes from the fire to Anata's and scowled. "She's too young," he stated, raising his voice slightly.

Suddenly, Merryn threw back the tapestry and burst into the room, her face glowing with light from the fire. "Too young for what?" she questioned, looking demandingly at her guardians.

Both Tarquin and Anata whipped their heads in her direction, wearing a mixture of anger and dread upon their faces. Tarquin spoke first.

"Merryn, go back to bed. We will discuss things after we've all had proper rest."

Displeased with his response, she looked pleadingly at Anata for aid. She made no reply but simply rested her arm behind Tarquin. They both stared motionlessly back at her, neither one saying anything more. Merryn could feel the anger boiling up inside her cheeks, and she screamed suddenly, "Why are you treating me as if I am a child? Have I not done everything you've asked of me? I am a *Swordwielder*, am I not? I could be second! I am your daughter!" She was crying.

All at once, the emotions from the last few weeks came bubbling to the surface like molten lava, scourging the earth. Yet inside, she felt only a vast emptiness. The frustrations from her past spun around her—the whirling images made her want to vomit. She needed answers—but to questions she didn't know she needed to ask. She stared back at the two in front of her. Anata's sad eyes caught her gaze first. She had never once seen Anata cry, nor had she ever wanted to, especially if it were her words that drew the tears.

Looking once again to her husband's council, Anata shot him a troublesome look and nodded solemnly.

Tarquin, who had said nothing else after Merryn's outburst, looked toward his wife, then back at Merryn. The anxiety from earlier now filled his face.

"Merryn, sit down."

Anger again began to rise; but before she could voice it, Tarquin repeated calmly, "Please, sit down."

She moved her way across the room and took a seat opposite her guardians. Her mind was buzzing. Tarquin walked away from the fire but resumed his usual stance. Anata remained seated on the hearth.

"Where would you like to start?" he asked calmly.

Merryn thought carefully for a moment before speaking. There was so much she didn't know—so much she didn't know she needed to know. Everything seemed so complicated. Letting her weight fall beneath her, she sank back and allowed the warmth of the fire to envelop her. She closed her eyes. Soon she was aware of a smooth hand caressing her cheek. *Anata*, she thought.

"It's all right, sweetheart. I know everything seems… confusing, and you're right to be angry." She sighed deeply before continuing, "Anger can seem like the right path, but it can only take you so far." She was looking intently toward Merryn. "Before we can tell you anything, something you must understand is that it was all done for your safety, child. Everything you've been through and will continue to learn was all for love."

At these last words, Merryn opened her eyes and found both of her guardians seated before her. Her face relaxed as she straightened her position in her seat. She placed her hands gently upon her lap and looked down, considering her first question. She so badly wanted to ask the question they'd been avoiding for fifteen years, but a more pressing concern was looming in the air—one that could change Tlogluck significantly in only a few days.

After several seconds passed, she looked to Tarquin and asked, "Who are the they? Why have they come so close to Tlogluck?"

Before he answered, he turned to look at Anata. Her eyes were filled with dread but remained strangely peaceful. "It's time," she said quietly to her husband.

Tarquin drew a long deep breath and took the seat nearest Merryn, gazing keenly into her eyes. "You must know if I tell you these things, you will not be the same. Anata and I, this village, everything you've known—it will all change. Are you ready for that?"

Merryn took in his words slowly, meditatively, and said firmly, "I think I've known for a long time now."

Tarquin stared down at her, his lips pursed into a sad smile. Though he was seated, his enormous body still towered over her, like the protector that he was. After a moment's pause, he stood and held out his hand toward Merryn, saying, "Then follow me."

"Where are we going?" Merryn asked wondrously.

He glanced at her admiringly, though still surging with apprehension. "I need to show you something."

The Secret Prisoner

The darkness had settled in the night sky above, but the stars remained scarce. Another blistering wind threw itself over the mountains and across the Crystal Lake as Merryn followed closely behind Tarquin. He had yet to tell her where they were going, but something inside her knew she was drawing nearer and nearer to answers, perhaps some she would soon wish she didn't know. Still, she followed.

They passed the Gathering Hall, where it seemed only moments ago she was to be announced as in the running for Second. However, the news of invaders quickly broke everyone into frenzy. There was a part of her that was no doubt grateful for the halt, as now she could perhaps refuse the position and seek to fill in the missing pieces of her memory. Yet there was another side that longed for the simplicity of a life in Tlogluck—one that, if she continued to follow Tarquin, would be lost. Still, as firm as the pull she felt for that life, the yearning for truth pulled at her heartstrings even more. She had to know the truth, about herself, her past. And whatever Tarquin was keeping from her was the key. She would continue at any cost; she must.

As they continued on foot, Merryn began to suspect they were headed for the Historia, which was on the far end of the village.

Nearing the entrance, Merryn suddenly got the notion that they were meeting Tribune Casca, and she would be forced to listen to one of his great oratories about the four realms. But as Tarquin pushed aside the grand door of the Historia and motioned her inside, that notion was suppressed at the feeling that what she was about to see was beyond even Casca's realm of reason.

The room was dark, darker than usual, as the massive chandeliers were not lit, leaving the old books and scrolls to the gloom of nightfall. She followed Tarquin passed the rows of tables where she imagined young principles sitting attentively earlier that day. Others, much like herself at that age, struggled to remain awake as they listened to ancient histories.

Strolling past the enormous aisles of bookshelves, lining almost the entire back end of the building, they reached what must have been Casca's study. No principle dared come this far into the Historia for fear of what tragic fate awaited them if Casca found them snooping. Tarquin pushed open the heavy wooden door; but before entering, he cast one last glance at Merryn, as if pleading for her to change her mind. Nodding firmly, she motioned for him to continue.

The room was hidden in the darkness, but Merryn prepared herself to see a large writing desk full of quills and rolls of freshly bound parchment, a typical fashion for the Lorefolk tribune. However, when Tarquin lit a small flame on the wall opposite Merryn, she was shocked at the seeming emptiness of the room. No desk, no quills or scrolls, just a small chamber, lined in moss-covered stone, that smelled faintly of something unpleasant. On the wall just beneath the rusted metal sconce appeared to be a strange symbol, carved into the stone. It was simple in detail, a circle made up of several smaller ones with arcs curved around each of them. It created a sort of winding effect. Merryn had studied runes in her principles but had never seen this one before.

Tarquin approached her slowly and whispered in her ear, "Do not be afraid." His voice was calm and stable, but his eyes gave off another sensation entirely. Confused at his statement, Merryn gazed at her adoptive father questioningly, but he gave no explanation. He merely turned and faced the wall in front of them and, placing his hand upon the stone symbol, pressed it inward. At first, nothing seemed to happen; but all of a sudden, a deep rumbling noise was heard as the stones in front of them began to break free from the wall, revealing a narrow passageway. Merryn's eyes grew large as Tarquin beckoned her closer. The passageway housed a small stone stairwell, which produced a faint light from below. Merryn looked to Tarquin who pushed forward, signaling for her to again follow. As they spiraled down around the staircase, the odor from before began to grow in strength. Nearing the bottom, Merryn covered her nose with her arm and whispered to Tarquin, "What is that smell?"

"You will know for yourself in a moment. Stay quiet." He led the way down the staircase, saying nothing else. Fortunately, the deeper the passageway led them, the brighter the light from below grew; and when Merryn thought they could descend no lower, they reached the bottom. The stench was nearly unbearable.

Tarquin halted suddenly and took a deep breath before moving to the side. Merryn's eyes scanned the room, noticing a vast number of wielders surrounding the large chamber's perimeter. They all seemed to be gazing at something in the far corner, covered in darkness. Before her eyes could adjust to the faint light, the other members of the tribunal came forward, wearing equal looks of outrage and bewilderment. Casca spoke first.

"Tarquin, what is the meaning of this?"

Tribune Margo spoke up from behind him. "Yes, Tarquin, she is a mere child. There is no need."

Their protests continued until Tribune Sophia stepped forward and stated, "I am sure, Tribunes, that Tarquin has rightful cause to bring young Merryn here tonight." She drew closer to Merryn, eyeing her suspiciously. "After all, this is the first time an invader has neared our borders in a decade. Our people are due an explanation."

"Enough, Sophia, please. In due time, all will be revealed. In the meantime, let me disclose to my daughter what I can in my own time." He glared at the other tribunes, who made no attempt to conceal their displeasure with Tarquin's statement. "For now," he said, looking to Merryn, "let's start with this." He gestured to the far end of the chamber, where something seemed to hold their attention. He motioned her forward to where her eyes could just make out a body in the faint light. Merryn squinted her eyes to see through the darkness. She had found the source of the stench.

Its skin was as black as pitch but seemed to be covered in rough bumps across the surface. Its face was covered in what appeared to be a smooth metal casing, slits for the mouth and nose only. The metal helmet covered his eyes, as if it were made in this fashion—for someone who couldn't see or rather *shouldn't* see. As Merryn eased forward, the creature gave a bloodcurdling growl and rocked from side to side. It was then that Merryn noticed the chains that bound him to the chair. Everyone bounded backward, and the wielders closest to the monster drew their swords.

"An invader," she stated plainly. "Tarquin, why are his eyes shielded?" Merryn turned her gaze to Tarquin, her mouth trembling in fear of his answer.

Tarquin glared at the monster before them and, without looking at Merryn, said, "It is a Charred One, Merryn. Its kind burns from within because of the evil in their hearts. They seek to bring out only the darkness within us all. That is why we must keep his eyes covered—because it *mustn't* see. They can see through us, down to our deepest desires."

Merryn suddenly thought of the blindfold from their sparring elites. *For use when sight is not possible*, she thought. "What if they find darkness—inside?" she asked.

"Then we become one of them." His words seemed to echo across the walls of the chamber. No one spoke a word.

Merryn's eyes flooded with the impending terror. "Hh—how do we stop them?" Her voice began to quiver, revealing the fear she struggled to hide.

Merryn glanced around the room at the many Swordwielders lining the walls, most of them strong and confident from years of training. A few, she noticed, were younger and seemed as fearful as she of the chained creature. As her eyes examined those of the other wielders, her gaze fell on one more familiar—a pair of dark eyes gazing back at her. *Brannick*.

What was he doing here? She knew he was a couple of years older, but he had only just completed his training—the same as Merryn. Brannick released his gaze from Merryn and rested them fixedly on Tarquin. Their eyes met; and sensing the questions arising in his adoptive daughter, he placed his hand behind Merryn and motioned her back to the stairway.

Merryn attempted to resist but was unsuccessful. "But—"

Tarquin interjected quickly, "Come. There is much to discuss, and here is neither the place nor I the one to explain. Come, Merryn."

He led them back up the stairwell, through the small chamber, and out of the hall of the Historia. Merryn thought her head might explode from all of the questions she faced. Alas, to find answers—but ones leading only to more questions.

As they started up the road toward the Gathering Hall, the sun slowly began its way over the peaks of the Shadowed Mountains. Anata met them by the entrance and gave Tarquin a sad smile. He disappeared inside, leaving the two women alone.

Anata wrapped her arms tightly around Merryn and pulled her close. "Come. Let's have a walk," she said.

The Awakened Answers

THE TWO HAD WALKED A mile before either spoke a word. As Merryn knew their destination, directions were unnecessary. Silent sobs escaped her mouth as tears trickled down her cheeks. Before long, they had arrived at her haven.

The Ridge was beautifully still during this time of day. The fresh morning awoke a peaceful quiet, as if everything but the horizon was still asleep. The village stood tranquil, as nature pulsed in its final flourishing moments before the bustle of life took over. Beauty, in all of its natural simplicity, resonated fully in this small valley. Here on this steep ledge, now more than ever, Merryn longed for peace amongst the chaos running rampant in her mind.

Anata sighed deeply and breathed in the cold mountain air. "I love this place." Her sincere tone echoed from the depths of her soul. "I was born here, you know. And all the time I was gone, I dreamed of the day I was to return home. I never dreamed I'd be returning with you." She smiled and playfully nestled her shoulder against Merryn's.

Merryn knew Tlogluck was where both Anata and Tarquin were raised. She knew they had left when they were much younger, but she never knew why nor why they had returned. She thought about the tales Tarquin would recite when she was a small child—mere stories to get her to sleep, she thought. Though now, a gleam of hope led her to find truth in them.

"'Nata, why did you leave?" For the first time since they'd left Tarquin in the village, Merryn gazed into her adoptive mother's eyes, the only mother she knew, until recently.

Anata smiled, and her eyes narrowed slightly as she peered off into the sun, rising over the eastern peaks. The silhouette of the mountains, outlined by the shades of bright gold and crimson, shadowed the small village below. It was this very moment for which the mountains were named and so enraptured the two women on the Ridge.

"Do you remember the history of the four realms?" asked Anata, still gazing off into the horizon.

Merryn, a look of puzzlement staunching her gaze, replied snidely, "Aye… but what does that have to do with the question?"

Anata let out a small chuckle and replied, "Patience, Merryn." She reached for the blonde streak in Merryn's hair and twirled it around her finger, smiling amusingly. "Do you remember why the Mover created the mountains?"

Merryn thought for a moment, staring out over the still water of the Crystal Lake. "As a symbol of endurance—to keep going when you feel as though you can no more," she replied plainly, almost mockingly.

"Aye, but not just as a symbol of physical stamina. The mountains are there to remind us of the enduring spirit that is to guide our very being. They represent just one element of the Stoneclad. We are to carry it with us… It is this that lasts when our bodies fail."

With her hands, Anata began tracing the outline of the glowing peaks in the horizon as she continued. "The mountains have a way of bringing that strength to the surface. It's that very reason I believe the Mover entrusted you to me. You, dear Merryn, are a treasure. You keep fighting even when you don't see the very thing which you are after. That's a gift only the Mover provides—the gift to press on while bearing the heaviest of burdens. That"—she added, pointing to Merryn's heart—"is something which cannot be taught."

Merryn gazed at her, questioningly. Anata simply smiled and continued, "You'll also be familiar with the name Halvor, then?"

She nodded. "They were the king's line. The guardians of the Stoneclad descended from the four heirs of the king." Merryn's voice heavy with a tone of annoyance.

"Very good—" Anata's reply was quickly interrupted by Merryn's growing frustration.

"You don't mean to tell me you are a Halvor, do you? There haven't been true guardians in a century. Casca said the line died long ago."

Anata laughed pensively. "Hmmpp. The wise tribune may be correct. But what you seem to have forgotten, dear child, is what happens when there are no true heirs."

Merryn, whose gaze was distracted by the shuffling of a snow owl in the trees behind them, suddenly shifted her gaze back toward Anata. Her face was aghast with disbelief. "You mean, you—"

"Yes." Anata continued, smiling brilliantly, "Long ago, I was appointed by the king as representative of the Mountain Realm, in the place of a rightful heir. I, along with three others, served as protectors of the Stoneclad in its home in Ignisia, the great fire city. The king had but two children when his young wife died, ending the hope of true guardians through his reign, and so there I remained until his son, King Hadrian, ascended, bringing new hope to the realms."

"King Hadrian—" Merryn paused briefly, considering Anata's words. "That would mean you were there when—"

"When the last king of the four realms fell… along with his great city, Ignisia. Yes, I was there," she replied solemnly.

A bleak light of understanding began to encircle Merryn as she listened to her words. Her stomach began to wrench, making her knees buckle. Had she not been seated, she might have fallen over. Short gasps of air escaped from her mouth as she worked up the next question. "Anata"—her hands began to tremble—"where did you find me?"

She didn't answer but simply glanced up along the southern ridgeline, masking the tears Merryn knew were falling down her cheeks.

Merryn placed her hand softly on Anata's and asked imploringly, "'Nata, please tell me."

Taking another long breath, Anata straightened her back, regaining her usual impressive demeanor, saying, "Because King Hadrian had but three children, it appeared his line was not to complete the guardianship, leaving the Stoneclad once again vulnerable." She paused as if preparing herself for the next part. "Soon, one of its protectors, Demari, grew dark, sick with his own jealous pride. He allowed the darkness to overtake him, enfolding a piece of the Stoneclad in its evil."

"But what about you and the others from the realms? Couldn't you keep the realms safe?" Merryn interjected.

Anata continued, "As protectors, we have power given to us from the Mover but not the kind bestowed upon the true guardians and never without the completed Stoneclad. We were useless against him. Demari was changed. His power was dark. He rose up an army and allowed the fire to engulf Ignisia. He then murdered the king and queen. Tarquin and I escaped... with you."

"Me?" she replied. "I'm from the fire city?"

Anata gleamed, an air of pride filling her expression. "You are the daughter of King Hadrian and his beloved wife, Queen Calla."

Merryn sat there, unmoving. "I... I don't understand. I was one of the three heirs?"

Anata stared intently down at her. She shook her head slowly. "No child." She hesitated before adding, "You were the fourth."

Chills jolted across her body as the dream she'd had just hours before came rushing back to her. The woman on the bed... the hooded figure holding the infant... the three children... "I was the... It was me... I was the baby."

"Oh, my darling, you are so much more than you can imagine. You are the fourth and final heir to complete the Stoneclad. You are its rightful guardian—you and your brothers."

As these last words left Anata, Merryn looked out beyond the horizon, reaching for the far-off places and the people she knew but had never met. That feeling of emptiness she so longed to quench was never for nothing. She knew she didn't belong but never knew why… until now. She now knew of her mother's fate; but her brothers—they were alive.

Brothers. Merryn let the word circle around in her mind before rolling off the tip of her tongue. "My brothers—where are they? How do I find them?"

"There are many things, my dear, that I cannot tell you. There is much to be done which, I am afraid, you must do alone," Anata replied with a look of deep despair.

"The Charred Ones—they are from the darkness?" she asked Anata, who nodded grimly. Merryn thought deeply, considering elements of the story she'd just heard. "But if there are four of us, why wouldn't the Stoneclad awaken and protect the realms as before?" Merryn announced suddenly, remembering something from the Lorefolk history.

"The darkness had already taken so many, and you were a mere baby. You did not know who you truly are. Remember, Merryn, the power of a guardian cannot be taught. It is something that is felt, deep inside. It is a gift from the Mover—a gift you possess. But you have to uncover it for yourself. Then you must remind your brothers."

"Remind them? How is it they don't know?" Merryn looked to Anata and suddenly remembered the dream—*the thing that had been taken from them*. "I have to remind them."

"Yes, Merryn. We had to ensure their safety as well, and the more they knew, the more things they *remembered*—the more danger they were in." Anata gazed deeply into her eyes. "You are their only chance, *our* only hope to restore the Stoneclad and our lands."

"But how—" Merryn began to speak but was quickly interrupted by the sound of a loud horn. The two women turned rapidly toward the village below. They faintly saw mounds of people filing into the Gathering Hall in the middle of the village. They knew all too well what the sound of the horn meant; the tribunal was meeting. They'd made a decision—an important one.

The Tribunal

MERRYN FOUND HERSELF WALKING DOWN the main street of Tlogluck, her thoughts distracted by the events of the day. She felt Anata's strong hand slide gracefully into her own as they entered the large hall. It was bustling with members of the village tribes.

Unlike feasting times, the tribes were not scattered randomly amongst each other. Rather, the tables were arranged in four long rows along the hall, each member sitting according to his own tribe. The tribunal sat in four enormous chairs at the right end of the building, adorned in their traditional meeting robes. The long purple garbs draped from each tribune as if a tapestry from a wall. Tarquin always said he'd rather they hang him from the ceiling than insist in his wearing the dreadful thing. But as always, he was forced to consent and now sat, first chair to the right, Tribune Margo and Sophia to his right and left.

The great hearth was as usual ablaze with a roaring fire, which seemed to ease the rather tense atmosphere growing inside the Gathering Hall. Tribesman sat huddled in small bits along the tables, gossiping about the present news.

Merryn had a difficult time believing that the results of her elites were announced only the night before. It seemed as if ages had passed since they announced the invaders. As they moved slowly into the building, she and Anata parted ways. Anata went to sit amongst a group of wielder women around her age; Merryn spotted Cadence and Connor sitting around a few other wielders in their final year. She quickly bounded in their direction and stole the seat next to Marco. She bumped him playfully and teased him about the sparring match. They all exchanged smiles and quickly erupted into conversation about the meeting. Everyone was a bustle of excitement—all except Aiden, whom Merryn noticed was sitting a few seats down, grimacing more than usual.

Cadence caught her stare and, leaning over Connor, whispered, "Haven't you heard?"

"No. What is it?" replied Merryn.

This time, the answer came from Marco who chimed in, "Rumor has it that Brannick's been named second. Can you believe it? Brannick?"

"He's a repeater! That's never been done!" the small tanned Zuri exclaimed.

A sudden burst of jealousy shot through Merryn; and for the first time in her life, she wore the same grimace as Aiden. She quickly glanced up at Tarquin, who remained calm and poised in his purple drapes. As if reading her mind, he stared directly into her eyes. For a moment, she felt shame rise into her cheeks. Wasn't this what she wanted? She didn't want to be second; she was set on refusing the position if offered. Then why, now, was she so angry with her adoptive father? She had received a way out. Why was she so upset?

Before she had time to mull things over, Tribune Casca rose and walked to the center of where the four tribunes were seated. The meeting had commenced.

Casca raised his arms to quiet the crowd, then spoke in his customary nasally tone. "We have gathered you here this morning to discuss some rather crucial events that have recently taken place in our small village. There is no need to be alarmed, but rather I urge you all to be attentive to what the other tribunes have to say and do your part in preparing for the times ahead." As he said this, he eyed each of the tables distastefully before bowing to Tarquin, beckoning him to take the stand.

Tarquin returned a bow to Casca and thanked him for his words of encouragement. He then faced the audience and spoke in his most authoritative voice. "First, as I am sure many of you are anxious to hear, the news of invaders is, in fact, true." A series of loud reactions burst around the hall. Shouts of protests and muffled cries echoed throughout the room. Tarquin stood tall and continued firmly. "They were spotted last night in the lower valleys and are moving this way. We are not sure what they want nor why they have come so close to the valleys. But be assured our scouts have surrounded the perimeters, and we are more than prepared to defend this village against any attack."

Slowly, the commotion decreased as his words fell throughout the crowd. His voice always had a calming effect; even as a child, she could remember waking from a nightmare and running to Tarquin. He would scoop her up in his arms and tell her a story, and something in his voice soothed her spirit until she again drifted to sleep. His words held the same restoring calm now more than ever.

"Our ranks will push beyond our borders so as to keep as much of the battle as far from the village as possible, but we will also leave behind forces to surround the village. There should be no fear, but everyone should remain strong." He paused as the sincerity in his voice rang out.

"In the meantime, we must listen to Tribune Casca's words and do our part to aid in this fight. In a moment, we will all report to our tribal quarters and be dealt further instruction. But first, it is my duty as Swordwielder tribune to announce a rather important decision regarding our tribe." The entire hall fell to a hush.

"It has been decided, resulting from the conclusion of wielder elites, that the position of second has fallen to Brannick Swordwielder." A succession of gasps and stifled applause filled the hall as Brannick appeared and took his place next to Tarquin.

"Brannick has proven himself worthy of this role countless times, and I am confident in my decision." As he made this statement, a few boys in their fourth year whispered something, no doubt about his repeating. Tarquin eyed them accusingly and continued, addressing the entire room, "You will all show him the proper respect due a wielder second." So saying, one by one, each table began to rise and subsequently bow their heads in tribute to the new second.

Merryn shifted in her seat as she rose to pay her respects. She looked down the table at Aiden, who appeared as if he would remain seated, then hesitantly stood along with the others. After a solemn moment, the room returned to their seats, and Tarquin continued, "Now, everyone is to report to his quarters and await instruction."

The whole room, apart from the Earthbearers who remained seated, piled noisily out of the hall doors as they made their way to their appointed buildings. The Lorefolk filed to the left toward the Historia, while the Euphony hung a sharp right in the direction of the gallery. The Swordwielders made for the sparring field, located just behind the Gathering Hall.

Once on the field, Tarquin appeared with Brannick, trailing closely behind him. Merryn felt her stomach flip with envy. She did not understand Tarquin's decision; she thought for sure that she would be named second. But again, each time she felt this way, another part of her flooded with relief. Seeing Anata near the back of the crowd, she began to push her way through gathering wielders to take her stance nearest her guardian.

Tarquin stood in front of the wielder front, preparing to relay orders. He began reemphasizing what he'd mentioned in the Gathering Hall before, adding, "For now, Brannick will assign you all duties. Most of you will resume your posts along the village perimeter. Others will join me in pushing toward the outlying borders. Principles will stay behind, filling in duties among other tribes. I will have no further discussion. Brannick will have your full attention." At these words, he stepped aside, allowing Brannick to take over his post and begin assigning positions.

Merryn began to inch her way toward the front in order to hear her assignment when she felt a sharp tug on her arm, pulling her backward. It was Tarquin. He leaned in closely and whispered in her ear, "It's my turn. We need to talk."

*****

"Are you angry with my decision?" he asked her, his eyes filled with concern. They were walking along the southern edge of the village, just before the main entrance. Assuming they would take a turn upon reaching the gate, Merryn was surprised to see Tarquin pull one of the tall structures open and usher her outside. Adding to her shock, awaiting the two of them outside of the gate was Tarquin's stallion Reinhold and Merryn's own Bruno.

"Where are we going?" Merryn asked as she stepped atop her horse. Stroking Bruno's blonde mane, she pensively stared off in the direction of the lake.

"Just for a ride," he said as he mounted his solid black stallion. "I thought we could survey the boundaries while we talk." Tarquin had not forgotten the question he asked earlier and continued to stare after Merryn, assuring her of that fact. To be such a strong man on the outside, Anata always said that he was mush on the inside, especially when it came to Merryn. This was one of those rare occasions where he let it show.

They had been riding for only a short distance when Merryn decided he had suffered enough. "I am not angry with you." She paused for a moment, thinking what she might say next. "I believe Brannick will make an excellent second."

"But—" he added, nudging for more information.

"But I am confused as to why he was chosen over myself. I've worked twice as hard as any in my year, and if anyone deserves this position, it's me." She began to hear her complaints as that of a child, and she felt the blood rush to her cheeks as she blushed.

Tarquin listened to her complaints without protest until she finished. "Did you want it?" he asked, though knowing full well her answer. She gazed back at him guiltily, his notion confirmed.

"Brannick repeated his elites and stilled scored on top," he said matter-of-factly. "Wouldn't you agree that counts as something?"

Merryn shrugged slightly; she hadn't thought about repeating in that light. Late-night sparring with Tarquin and extra recitations paled in comparison to repeating those grueling days. Merryn exhaled deeply before saying, "Then why did he repeat? If he was to be second, why did he have to do them again?"

Tarquin looked off in the distance and exhaled loudly as he said, "Because I asked him to."

Her head jerked rapidly toward Tarquin, pulling Bruno's reins with her; he gave a quick jump before settling down once more. Her eyes were large with shock. "What? Why would you do that?"

He took a deep breath and narrowed his eyes toward the distance. "You were thirteen when we first heard news of raids in the valleys of the foothills. You needed protection, Merryn, and Brannick showed great promise of becoming tribune someday. I promised him the position of second if he agreed to stay behind and keep an eye on you. He has orders that if anything were to happen to Anata or myself, then he is to take you away."

"So he knows about me—about who I am?" she asked him.

Tarquin shook his head. "Not everything—just that you're… very special." He smiled. "He didn't need much convincing."

Merryn thought back to her time with Brannick. She hadn't really known him during their principles, as he was several years ahead of her. But when he failed his elites. *But he hadn't failed, not really*, she thought. *Why would he agree to go through that, all of the humiliation? Was becoming second or perhaps tribune so alluring that he'd agree to fail his elites for a guaranteed spot?*

Merryn reflected on these things for a moment before adding, "It's amazing what people will undergo for the sake of power." She glanced off into the horizon, shaking her head in disbelief.

Tarquin nodded. "Among other things."

Merryn turned again to look at Tarquin, who was wearing a slight smile. "What do you mean?" she asked.

Tarquin didn't answer but merely replied with another question, "What do you think of Brannick?"

Merryn gaped at him, her face a picture of bewilderment. "What do I think of… Brannick?" She stopped to consider his question as her lips contorted into a scowl. Continuing, she said, "Well, I can't say I really know him. From all appearances, he's rude, conceited. He's just like Aiden—" She paused abruptly to reconsider as Tarquin gaped her with disbelieving eyes. "Okay, well, maybe not *just* like Aiden. I mean, I think he will make for a good second and perhaps tribune… one day. Why do you ask?"

"Just curious," he said with a smile as he nudged Reinhold forward.

They continued on their ride until the sun appeared directly overhead, and they decided to head back for midday feast. As they drew near to the gate, two young wielders approached to tend to the horses. She and Tarquin dismounted and passed the reigns off to the boys before pushing through the gates. The snow, piled along the sides of the main road, was beginning to melt; and the day seemed warmer than most. Merryn felt Tarquin pull her toward him, and she wrapped her arms around his large frame. Neither noticed, but both were smiling as they made their way toward the Gathering Hall.

THE SURGING FLAME

UPON COMPLETION OF MIDDAY FEAST, the tribes left the Gathering Hall with full stomachs and lighter hearts. Given the present circumstances, it might be more customary to have a quick meal and return to posts; however, Tribune Margo thought it more pleasing to make a crowd favorite for lunch and conclude with some lighthearted medleys from Tribune Sophia and other members of the Euphony. The result was most pleasing to all who then left feeling refreshed and ready to continue with their assigned tasks.

Anata had not been in the hall as she and several other women from the other tribes had taken to the fields to provide lunch for the wielders on post. Because Merryn had left before being assigned her own post, she and Tarquin walked to their lodging to see if Anata had yet returned. As they passed the other dwellings along the road to theirs, Merryn imagined she would be assigned a post somewhere near the village, considering the newly discovered circumstances in which she was under.

She had not had time enough to consider what this now meant for her here in the village. Anata had mentioned that she would have to leave to find her brothers, but she had no idea of their names or even where to start. She thought about the name she had for so long been under, Swordwielder. No one had a true last name in the village of Tlogluck; rather everyone was named according to their tribe. Because she had not changed tribes after principles, her last name remained the same… until now.

Halvor—the name sounded so strange to her, so foreign. Yet just as the idea that she was meant for much more than Tlogluck encompassed her thoughts, the name grew more and more familiar with every breath. She glanced up at Tarquin as they made their way through the village streets. He looked so certain as he glided down the muddy roads, soaked from melting snow.

Suddenly, a pit fell into her stomach as she considered what this meant for him. This man, who had raised and cared for her as his very own, was now faced with the truth that she was not really his. She had been so angry with him for weeks now, as her heart swam with the truth that she now knew but strived to understand. She had not considered anyone else's feelings, especially Tarquin's. Merryn felt tears well up in her eyes as she stopped in the middle of the road. Tarquin gave a quick leap as he bounded back to her place in the street. Gently placing both hands on either side of her delicate frame, he sunk down to his knees to look his daughter in the eyes.

"Merryn, what is it? What's wrong?" he looked pleadingly in her eyes. She didn't want to hurt him anymore than he was already, but she knew her next words would bring only that. So she remained quiet, crying silently in his strong, dark arms. Again, he pleaded, "Merryn, please tell me. What can I do?"

"Be my father," she whispered through muffled sobs.

Tarquin's eyes grew large with understanding of her statement. The truth that they had been keeping from her since her birth now resonated deeply in his own heart. "Merryn," he said quietly, and looking around him, he stood and pulled Merryn in an alley between two homes. He then resumed his position in front of her and gazed fixedly into her eyes.

Brushing away the tangles of her blonde streak from her face, he continued saying, "Knowing who you are makes me love you no less. The name you bear makes no difference to me or to Anata. You are our daughter because we *choose* to love you as such. Do you understand this?"

She glanced up at his tough features, his face stern and rugged, but she heard only the sincerity in his voice. She nodded slowly.

Tarquin smiled slightly back at her and wiped a single tear from her eye. "Do you know why I have been so hesitant to tell you these things?"

Merryn sniffed and reclined against the wall of the dwelling. "Because I am too young. I'm not ready to leave."

"No, my darling child." He gazed at her intently as he said, "Because you *are* ready, and that means you will *have* to leave. Anata and I have known for some time now, but I needed more time with you—for my own sake." He paused as he took a seat next to her beside the wall. "Merryn, I cannot express to you the depths of my love for you and your mother. I was so afraid when we brought you here. I knew who you were and what that meant for us, but that is all I knew. I didn't know what the tribunal would say or do. I told them we found you outside of the valley and that we would be raising you as our own." Then turning to face her, he said, "Merryn, that is why I trained you the way I did—why I always pushed you to be the best. Because I knew what you had to do, for your family, for all of us. I promised Anata that I would do everything to keep you safe—"

His statement was cut short as Merryn leaped across him, throwing her arms around his broad shoulders. They remained there for several moments before he leaned forward and came to a standing position, his adoptive daughter still wrapped tightly in his arms. Her feet dangled several feet from the ground before he slowly placed her back down. She stared up into Tarquin's eyes, her own gleaming brightly. "'Nata's, right," she said. "You *are* mush!"

They exchanged humorous glances before turning to walk toward their dwelling. As they drew closer, they noticed a tall slender figure walk inside, the door held open by Anata, who rapidly motioned them forward. Without another glance at each other, they took off running.

*****

When they entered inside, they found Anata standing by the door and Tribune Sophia, hooded, standing next to the hearth. It took Tarquin only a moment to shake his fatherly affection and regain his tribunal composure.

"Sophia, what is the meaning of so informal a greeting? Has everyone in your tribe found the necessary areas in which to fill?" he said authoritatively.

"Yes, Tarquin, we are more than capable of tending to needs when necessary," she said with a tone of distaste.

"Then there are disputes among your tribe in their tasks? I cannot imagine another reason you would allow for such a meeting in my own home." Tarquin's manner quickly shifted, gaining a sense of irritation that made Merryn feel a bit uncomfortable.

"Do not play coy with me, Tarquin. You know my purpose here." Sophia spit her words so forcefully that her graceful, feminine demeanor faded into that of the resilient tribune she was. "A force of Charred Ones will be upon us in a matter of days, and I have a right to know why."

Merryn looked from Tarquin to Anata, who pursed her lips and took a seat next to the fire. She sighed heavily before saying, "She's right, Tarquin. It's time she know." Turning to Merryn, she held out her hand and motioned for her to take the seat beside her.

Tarquin closed his eyes and, dropping his head, walked forward. "Tribune, if you would, first, so kindly explain your vision to Merryn." His voice transformed to his usual firm, steady tone so suddenly that Merryn was startled by the rapid shift. She then fixed her gaze on Tribune Sophia, who was already eyeing her distrustfully.

"As you well know, Merryn, the Euphony are known for their gift of sight." She paused as Merryn knowingly nodded. She then continued by saying, "It is not always the most… reliable… of gifts. As when I am presented with a vision, it is often vague and appears… fragmented." With each hesitated word, she eyed Tarquin pointedly.

"However, many years ago, I received one vision that troubled me greatly. It occurred the very night you were brought into the village." She now turned and arched her neck directly toward Merryn. "Do you want to guess what I saw?"

Merryn shifted uncomfortably in her seat and answered, "I don't know, Tribune."

"I saw our village under siege, fire raging throughout as Charred Ones desecrated our home." Her voice began to shake and rise in volume. Tarquin moved forward.

Merryn stared back at her plainly, her mind whirling with questions. "I'm sorry, Tribune, but what does that have to do with me?"

Sophia pulled herself back and regained her position by the hearth. Several moments passed before she continued. "I also saw a girl—a strange girl wearing the crest of a Swordwielder. Now tell me—you are rather bright—what does this vision say to you?" She turned her head rapidly to face Merryn, whose eyes were now wide with terror.

"I—" She was about to speak when interrupted by another.

"They are not after Merryn!" It was Anata who spoke. Her voice resounded so vehemently everyone's gaze shifted to where she sat next to Merryn. Anata continued saying, "They are not after her. They do not know she even exists."

Sophia began to speak, but Anata quickly interjected, "You see Merryn in your vision because she is who they *need*, but this is unknown to their leader and must remain so."

Merryn looked to Tarquin, who stood off to the side, his eyes set firmly on Anata. The fear, exuding from his gaze, echoed the truth of her words.

"Then who?" Sophia asked determinedly.

"They are after me," Anata said, her voice retaining its natural calm. "They seek the remaining protectors of the Stoneclad. As far as I know, I am the only one left."

Merryn moved in her seat and, leaning toward her guardian, said, "But, 'Nata, why would they need you?"

"They seek me, Merryn, to kill me. As long as I am alive, a piece of the Stoneclad remains light, and the Dark Prince cannot contain it completely," she stated coolly.

"But the—you're not—the prince? 'Nata, I don't understand." Merryn's eyes again filled with dread, as tears fell once more.

"Shh, child. You do not understand now. But you will, soon." Anata placed her hand on the side of Merryn's face. "I told you there is much to learn."

As she calmed Merryn, Tarquin stepped in front of them, blocking Sophia's view, who until now gazed confusingly at the two women. Tarquin spoke in his most commanding tone. "I think it's time you leave now, Sophia. You've received your answer." He held his gaze on her firmly until she made her way toward the door. As soon as she opened it, a piercing scream shot through the village.

*****

Chaos filled the village as tribesman ran throughout the streets. Tarquin called for news from the nearest wielder.

A young man, not much older than Merryn, came close, terror filling his eyes. "A mass of Charred Ones were spotted not fifteen miles from Tlogluck. They will be upon the village by nightfall," he said.

Tarquin called for the meeting horn to blow, gathering the people together. Once everyone in the village had assembled in the Gathering Hall, Tarquin rattled instructions to the crowds:

"Everyone is to gather provisions and make way for the mountains. You are to take only what you can carry. Leave behind anything that would slow you or prevent you from climbing. Young wielders in years one through six will lead you up the trails. Wielders, it is your duty to protect them. Every trained Swordwielder of age will remain behind to fend off the horde of invaders. Do not fear them. If you doubt, keep your eyes closed. Remember your training. Now go!"

At these words, everyone in the hall scattered to the various positions. Merryn broke for the sparring fields but not before a massive fist grabbed hold of her arm yet again.

"Let me go!" she screamed. Whirling around, she saw Brannick, his eyes determined and unyielding, as he pulled her in the opposite direction, toward her home.

She kicked at him and tried to pull away, but he never adjusted his grip. Gritting his teeth together tightly, he said, "Stop kicking, Merryn! You have to come with me."

"Brannick, let me go!" As she said this, she let her foot fly up overhead, nailing him square in the forehead. His grip loosened, and she took off sprinting. This time, it was Anata who stood in her way. She appeared so suddenly that Merryn skidded to a stop, falling backward to the ground.

Anata spoke confidently. "Merryn, you are to go with him. He will take you to the borders, but then you must go on alone. Do you understand me?"

Merryn regained her footing and stood tall, her eyes mixed with anger and confusion. "No! I am not going anywhere! Anata, you just said they are after *you*! *You* are not safe here! Come with me," she pleaded.

"The longer they hunt for me, the more time you will have. There's no time to waste, Merryn. You must go."

"Where? Where do I go?" she exclaimed.

Suddenly, Brannick appeared again with two packs slung over his back; his dark arm reached across Merryn to hand one of them to Anata. Merryn gaped at him, confusingly. Anata began pushing her forward toward the gate. "You will go to the Deserts of Yehuda. That is the nearest realm. You should find your brother there."

As they moved, Anata pulled something small from beneath her own cloak and threw it into the pack Brannick had given her, before placing it securely across Merryn's back. "Do not be seen. Stay amongst the forest until you see them pass. Do *not* fight them," she said sternly, her gaze shifting between both of them.

Merryn's head spun with confusion. She had so many questions with no idea where to start, but one question resonated deeply as she said, "'Nata, who—who is he?"

"Thaddeus—look for Thaddeus. He is waiting for you," she said calmly.

Brannick nodded firmly and placed his arm behind Merryn, pushing her forward. She hesitated and, with a forceful turn, leaped for Anata, wrapping her arms tightly around her. "I love you," she said.

"Forever, my darling girl. Forever."

And they ran.

Part 4

THADDEUS

THE ESCAPE

THE SUN ADVANCED ITS WAY slowly into the desert sky, masking the chill of dusk with warm bursts of light. The tiny village, hidden amongst the dunes of the Yehuda Valley, stirred in a bustle of commotion as its inhabitants made hasty preparations for their departure. Makeshift shelters were being torn down as carelessly as they had been constructed. Tenants nosed through piles of decrepit materials with the hope of potential sales. The Trader tent, where scavengers like Bexler and his clan made their deals, was nothing more than a few useless scraps left in the sand; its residents, upon hearing the news of the impending raid, had up and gone hours earlier. The rest of the village was to hear news of the Charred Ones from travellers passing through.

Seeing as Bexler's clan had just nearly returned from the previous pillage, they had nothing left to gather but what remained in Bexler's cellar and a few *personal* items in their sleeping quarters. Thaddeus shrugged off a laugh as he thought about the personal items he owned. Nothing belonging to any clansmen was really his own, as Bexler would sell anything of value right from under him. With the exception of the engraved sketchbook Thaddeus now clutched firmly in his grip, he thought only of a few other things in his lodging.

Ever since he'd proven his usefulness with a pen years ago, Bexler always saw to it that Thaddeus had a sketchbook of some sort in order to wade in on any necessary transactions. The one he'd been using the previous night remained where he'd left it on his bed. Reaching down to retrieve it, he thumbed through some of the pages. Images of odd-looking contraptions, made from random scavenged goods, filled the majority of the book; a few contained sketches of people: Netheq, the twins, people from the village, and a couple of caricatures of Wormer with the body of a slithering worm, and of Bexler who appeared as a deformed gorilla. Then filling the corner spaces on some sheets and several pages toward the back of the book was the picture of the young girl who occupied what dreams he had. Several simple silhouettes covered the sides and corners, while other larger images filled entire pages. Though the shading and artistic techniques varied on several pictures, it was undeniably the same girl—the same dark hair but with one lighter strand framing her face. But the most striking detail was the intricacy of her eyes; Thaddeus spent the most time shading and shaping her eyes to capture the same detail and intensity he felt from them. He knew he'd never seen her before; and for a while, he dismissed the images as someone he'd merely imagined. Yet there was always a part of her that struck him as familiar, denying him the ease of dismissing her from memory. He must have known her, for his mind refused to let him forget.

Grabbing his pack from the corner of the room and stuffing it with a tunic and the animal hide from his bed, he placed the old sketchbook inside the new one and loaded them into his pack. Throwing his newly filled pack over his shoulder, he turned to walk out of the room when he heard the scream.

"Charred Ones! They are here!" a voice cried out from somewhere in the village.

Thaddeus tore through the remaining fragments of wood that once surrounded the traveller's lodging. Most of it had been pillaged by fleeing residents. All that was left were the tattered walls of the dormitories and the scraps of cloth used as doors. The village itself looked vastly different from earlier that morning. The shelters were down, wagons and cellars emptied, and the inhabitants were either gone or leaving, including his own convoy. Thaddeus glanced across the remains of the town for any sign of Bexler and the wagon. There, to the west, was a thick black line making its way briskly toward his direction. On the other side was a scattered mass of dots, quickly diminishing as the village residents dispersed in the opposite direction.

Suddenly, a gust of wind brought with it a blast of sand that encircled the camp. Squinting his eyes as the sandstorm rushed around him, Thaddeus could just make out the wagon he'd bartered for Bexler, trailing fast behind the fleet of villagers. A fat blob, which he knew to be his coward of a guardian, sat bouncing on its top. He knew he'd never catch up with them on foot, nor had he any other means by which to escape. His only option was to hide and pray to the Mover he would not be discovered. Perhaps once the Charred Ones noticed the vacancy of the camp, they'd march on; but Thaddeus knew that was wishful thinking. They nearly always left a burning trail of some kind.

Judging by the speed at which they moved, he assumed the raiders would be at the camp within the hour, giving him less time than he'd like to find a proper hiding place. The village was mostly desolate, aside from the dilapidated shelter that used to be his quarters and the few cellars that remained empty but intact. Neither of these would be of any use, as structures were typically burnt to the ground. His best bet was to stay as low to the earth as possible and avoid being trampled by their weight. *If only he could bury himself,* he thought half-heartedly. Suddenly, his eyes fixed on something a ways off in the distance but on the opposite side of the oncoming assailants. On the north end of the camp stood the village watering well. It wasn't large, no bigger than one of the wheels of Bexler's cart; but it was hidden behind the traveller's lodging, keeping it from the Charred Ones line of sight. The water had been slim, he knew; and he had no way of determining its depth. But the way he saw it, he had two options: falling in a seemingly bottomless well and quite possibly breaking all body parts before dying a slow death *or* fighting off a horde of Charred Ones. Whatever his choice, he had to make it soon, as either his mind was inventing some sick story, or he was, in fact, hearing fearsome growls from south of the camp. For a moment, he considered the latter option, as it might be faster; but he quickly shook off the notion as cowardice and decided he'd make for the well. With no more time to consider other alternatives, Thaddeus adjusted the straps on his pack, pulling them tightly across his body, and darted for the well.

The stones forming the perimeter of the well were caked with residue from camel spit and smelled of an odor oddly familiar to Bexler. Peering inside, the pit was too deep to see far below the surface; and for a second, he reconsidered his choice. As he took a second look inside the well, he pulled his pack closer, praying there would be water to catch his fall. Taking a deep breath and glancing back once more at the camp, he exhaled and jumped.

The Unexpected Guest

THE WELL WAS DEEPER THAN he'd hoped; but to his great delight, there resting at the bottom was nearly twelve feet of water. On the sides of the well were several small protrusions of metal, which thankfully he did not hit during his descent, and offered a small amount of support. His pack was mostly submerged under the water and became heavier with every second. He never imagined he'd be so happy to have his drawings ruined from the water, but the fact that he hadn't been crushed from the fall made it a welcomed notion.

The well was dark, and the broad daylight above provided only a small circle of light down into its depths. The width of the well was just beyond his arms' reach across, which would mean he'd be able to climb up when it was safe. *If it was safe*, he thought. He hadn't exactly thought that far ahead; he was merely trying to avoid being seen by the onslaught of invaders. Fortunately, he made good time as the sun had just crossed from overhead, removing the direct sunlight from the well's opening. Perhaps it would be dark before the Charred Ones even approached the well, and they would have no chance of seeing down.

Thaddeus attempted to shake from his mind the possibilities of what they might do to the well instead, and a forthcoming sense of dread filled his stomach. *One thing at a time*, he kept reminding himself.

He continued to stare upward, treading gently and resting on the metal brackets as often as possible. He counted as the minutes passed, then an hour. A ray of hope shone brightly when no noise came from the camp, disclosing any sound of an attack. *Maybe they had run right passed him*; and considering the thought, he braced himself to begin the ascent to the top.

Flipping over on his stomach, he reached his arms as far out in front of him as they could go and felt for the opposite wall with his feet. He was going to walk his way back up the stonewall. He took his first step upward and followed with his arm, alternating with each move. His pack was now saturated with water and weighed heavily upon his back. Soon, his body was nearly three feet from the surface of the water, and he inhaled deeply. Upon his exhalation, the sound of a small splash drew his attention to his left side. He drew in his breath and waited for another sound, as if to second-guess his sanity. Several seconds passed before another subtle ripple coursed through the water. He froze, and a feeling of terror shot through him, paralyzing his endeavor. He had not been alone in the well, and whatever was with him had been oddly silent the entirety of their time together. Whoever it was, he was not staying to find out.

Regaining his climbing pattern, he took another deep breath and began bouldering toward the top. He had not taken more than one step when he heard the water ripple underneath his body. It was swimming toward him. A faint cry released from his breath, revealing his terror of the unexpected guest. Panicking slightly, Thaddeus hurried his movements; but before he could take another step, a hand covered his mouth as he felt his body convulse and drop to the water with a loud smack. With his mouth still covered, the stranger pulled him close, their feet swimming furiously below. Thaddeus wanted to scream or bite or kick—anything to get away from what had him bound, but the idea that the stranger might try to drown him made him change his mind. Then a thought passed over him. Whoever was with him must have been trying to escape the Charred Ones as well—the reason for his silence, no doubt. No sooner had the notion crossed his mind than a strangely familiar voice hissed across his ears.

"Shhhh. Look." Had he been able to see in front of him, he would have noticed Netheq pointing his tattooed finger upward toward the opening. Thaddeus relaxed a bit and lifted his gaze, seeing nothing but a faintly graying sky. Then after a moment, something black appeared in the opening, a Charred One. Thaddeus stopped breathing entirely and went rigid in Netheq's grasp. The Charred One screamed something unrecognizable and tossed a piece of wood down to the bottom. Bouncing off the sides of the well, the scrap barely missed Thaddeus, splashing in the water just inches from his face. Another figure appeared in the opening and gazed down below. Afterward, it slapped its hand across the head of the other, releasing a vulgar scream as it did so. The second one walked away, but the first remained for another moment or two, staring down to the bottom. *Can it see us*, Thaddeus wondered. What happened next gave him his answer. A loud horn echoed through the camp and down to the depths of the well as the Charred One disappeared. They were leaving; whatever they'd done was finished.

THE ASCENT

SEVERAL MINUTES HAD PASSED BEFORE Netheq released his hold over Thaddeus's mouth and several more after that before either spoke a word. Finally, Thaddeus broke the silence.

"What are you doing here?" he asked probingly. "I thought you'd run off with Bexler."

He was answered with a stark silence.

"Did he leave you too?"

Again, silence. Thaddeus exhaled deeply and began to once again feel his way around the well.

"Well, I am going to try and get out of here," he said matter-of-factly. "You think it's safe?" he asked, not expecting a reply but merely hoping for some form of affirmation of his endeavor. Still, Netheq made no answer and swam backward, his back to the wall. Thaddeus sighed and resumed his climbing position.

He was clearly fatigued from treading water; and had it not been for the provision of the small metal protrusions jutting out from the walls, he might have sunk long ago. Fortunately, they provided just enough support to allow him rest, if only for a short period. After several failed attempts at scaling the walls, Thaddeus suddenly realized the extent of his fatigue and reached for one of the metal brackets, his breaths escaping in loud, rhythmic spasms. He was too tired to climb. The sky was gradually dimming above, expressing the fact that they'd been down there longer than he'd guessed. A sudden thought paraded his mind: *What if he can't get out? Was he to die down there?* All of these years surviving and he was going to die... in a well... with Netheq.

As the thought passed, Netheq made a sudden leap in the water. He landed spread-eagle against the walls of the well, his legs catching his weight on either side. Thaddeus watched in amazement as Netheq shuffled his way up the flanks. With each step, he simultaneously kept his balance with his hands, palms flat against the stone. Before the action truly resonated with Thaddeus, the tattooed man had reached the top and jumped out of the opening with ease.

Thaddeus stood, his mouth agape, staring at the strange man gazing down on him from above. Netheq took a final look, perhaps expecting him to make another effort. Thaddeus knew his strength was wearing thin but thought he'd give the climb one more try. He positioned himself for the ascent and slowly eased his way up. His pack, now soaked thoroughly, shifted to one side on his back. His grip loosened under the unbalanced weight, and he slipped. His body landed in the water with a resounding splash. He thought about the leather-bound sketchbook in his pack and the letter from Shamra that was undeniably ruined at this point. If he ever got out, maybe he could salvage what was left; but at the rate he was going, he might not ever have that option. He gazed up, expecting to see Netheq peering down on him; but he saw only gray sky. Netheq had given up and was undoubtedly long gone.

Thaddeus let out a disgruntled cry and sank back against the stone wall. He was tired; and though he didn't like to admit it, he was scared. *Calm down. You have to calm down*, he kept saying to himself. *Rest, just rest. You'll be fine.* His simple attempts at encouragement echoed in futile waves in the darkening pit. He closed his eyes and fought back the tears that were forcefully making their way out. He wondered how long it would take for someone to find him down there. They hadn't had rain in almost a year. These gruesome notions twisted his face into a grimace, and he forced them away.

Instead, he thought about something else—someone else. Instantly, the girl from his drawings filled his mind. She stared back at him with the eyes that he so expertly drew. She never failed to give him a sense of purpose. When he looked at her, it was as if he was looking into another life—one full of joy and meaning. For the first time all day, he was at peace.

Glancing toward the sky, now speckled with stars, he closed his eyes and said a prayer of thanks to the Mover. Just then, he heard a rustling noise from above and, opening his eyes, saw Netheq tossing something down to him. It was a rope.

*****

The wide assortment of escapees from the trader village spread across the vast desert like ants across a trampled hill. Rickety wagons, worn down from the desert sands, creaked and groaned as their drivers wheeled them along the dust-laden tracks. Grungy camels and mules hung their heads low to the ground in utter exhaustion from the hasty evacuation.

Bexler and his crew of scavengers held fast in their wagon. Wormer, who sat dangling his legs off the back, struggled to keep his eyes open for any sign of the Charred Ones. The twins sat back to back in the middle, between Wormer and Bexler. Their eyes opened and closed every so often as they took turns sleeping. It was a most bizarre image to behold. When one's eyes appeared to be shut, the next minute they'd be wide open and on full alert, while his brother, who was awake only moments ago, now appeared fast asleep. Bexler was poached high atop the wagon in his usual position of authority, bouncing to and fro as poor Al Haml the camel lugged them on.

They had been traveling along this road for several hours but were still quite a distance from their destination, about which none of them knew. Making for another village was pointless, as that would lead to a repeat of the past few hours; but they had to find some kind of hideout and wait for the raid to pass through.

The smartest thing would be to egress from the Charred Ones' path and travel north or south; and though Bexler was not the brightest of beings, he knew well enough to stick to the desert roads. Several travelers in their convoy of escapees decided that a southern route to the border of the Sidon Sea would be preferable than their current path. Bexler simply released a grisly laugh and watched them go, happy to have lessened the number of travelers. Having been a scavenger for many years, Bexler knew all too well what awaited wanderers who strayed from the desert path and was not about to be one of them.

"Where do ya suspect their headin'?" asked Wormer, his face drawn up in an exhausted gaze.

"No clue," replied Bexler. "Me guess is the mountains, in which case we best not be travelin' much further in this direction, boys."

"Where do we go then, Bex?" Wormer turned, wearing a mixture of fatigue and confusion, and faced his boss. A great yawn escaped from his mouth as he stretched his skinny arms high overhead.

Bexler rolled his eyes, staring straight ahead, and said with a tone of annoyance, "If I knew that, don't ya think I'da told ya already?"

By now, the twins had both opened their eyes and were wide awake, gazing off on either side of the wagon. Wormer let out an exasperated sigh and regained his position on the back of the wagon, alternating his feet the way a small child might do.

A few minutes passed when Wormer again piped up, asking, "What ya think is up in them mountains?"

Bexler contemplated the question for another moment before replying, "Nuttin' I want comin' down. It's a strange place, them mountains, full of all kinds of tricksies. Anythin' they want from up there, they can have." His voice trailed off as he gazed ahead of him. In the distance stood the lofty Shadowed Mountains. Snow clouds were gathered around its stiff peaks. Wormer lay his head against the wood railing of the wagon and shut his eyes, allowing the last few days' fatigue to fall over him.

As the sun began to set in the western horizon, their convoy, having decreased to just one rickety crate with wheels, dragged on alone down the worn path. They were approaching the eastern dunes, which marked the boundaries to the foothills of the mountains. There they could set up camp and rest for the night. Bexler pulled the wagon behind a high dune—stopping with so sudden a jolt that Wormer fell off of the back.

"Oy! What ya do that for?" he cried, wiping the sand from his face.

Bexler wailed in an obnoxiously high-pitched voice, "Oh, I'm sorry, lad. Did ya want me to come and wake ya up like ya mammy and pat yer skinny littl' head?" He hobbled over to Wormer and swatted him hard across the skull before saying, "Now set up camp. I'm starvin'."

Wormer rubbed the side of his head and mumbled something incomprehensible. The twins pulled some sticks of firewood and a packet of dried meat from the wagon. Mierisch began stacking the twigs for a fire, while Hanoch tossed the dried meat to Wormer.

"What am I supposed to make with this?" he complained. Hanoch simply stared back at him, eyeing him insouciantly. Wormer had been allowed to tag along, partly because he had an odd knack at making what little food they had edible, but mostly because he came with Al Haml, who had now nearly fallen over from exhaustion.

Bexler walked over by the small fire and threw himself onto a rug of sheepskin. "You ain't supposed to make anythin' from it, you idiot. You're supposed to eat it."

Wormer eyed the bag suspiciously then, shrugging his shoulders, replied coolly, "Oh. Right." He joined the disheveled bunch by the fire, tore off a piece of the meat, and threw the bag to Bexler. They chewed and spit and spoke seldom before all four men were passed out next to a smoky pile of ash.

Then they heard the snarls.

THE BURNING

THE FOUR MEN SPRANG FROM the ground in a whirl of panic. They hadn't intended on sleeping very long, but the events of the last days got the best of them. Hurriedly, they gathered up what belongings they had and made a dash for the wagon. Wormer pulled at Al Haml's harness, but he wouldn't budge; he was too tired to move.

"Come… on, you stubborn beast!" Wormer gritted his teeth as he pulled on the harness and yelled at Al Haml, who simply lay back down, oblivious of the impending doom. "Oy… he's not budgin," he called after Bexler, who then stomped his way to the camel. As he began to lift his foot to kick the animal, another loud rumble was heard just on the other side of the dune. It was too late; they were here.

Bexler jolted suddenly, turning his head toward the road just behind the dune. The four men crouched down behind the wagon. Each one wore a look of outright terror. Perspiration dripped from Bexler's head and down his face as he peered over the side. Then, as if running directly into him, the smell hit them. Each man covered his face with his arm, trying to mask the sound of the gags brought from the stink. Rotting, burning flesh filled the dunes around them as a horde of Charred Ones marched past their position.

The smell so disturbed Al Haml as well because he shot up and darted north. His exit caught the attention of a couple of the creatures running past, who pointed in his direction but maintained their course.

"Al Haml!" cried Wormer in a muted voice as he stood up to follow his camel. Bexler suddenly grabbed him by the vest and jerked him back down.

"Not yet, you idiot! They're still here!" He glared at him until Wormer turned around, wearing a disgruntled frown, and noticed several other Charred Ones piling past the opening between the dunes. Several moments passed before anyone made a sound. When it looked as if no more Charred Ones would pass, Bexler motioned to the twins, who ran ahead to the opening. Bexler made his way to the top of the bank and peered over; Wormer followed close behind.

Hanoch walked up the path a ways in the direction of the raiders. He paused briefly and said in his foreign dialect, "They head for the foothills. The mountains are their aim." His eyes gazed up toward the cliffs of the mountain as he spoke. Bexler grunted and began to head back toward the wagon, pulling Wormer along with him.

Mierisch bent down, examining a pool of black ooze puddled in the sand prints. He sniffed it and winced in disgust, the smell again filling his nostrils. Glancing up, he noticed his brother had turned to face him, but his eyes were set with horror. Mierisch rose slowly from the ground, eyeing his brother questioningly. Then suddenly, a familiar roar filled in around them as Mierisch soon bore the same petrified gaze as his brother. As he slowly turned around, in front of him stood one of the beasts, a Charred One, left behind to retrace their route.

Mierisch froze with terror, words unable to escape his lips. The Charred One reached out its black hand, oozing with sores, and caught hold of Mierisch's neck. It lifted him up so as to gaze into his eyes. The twin was paralyzed. After several seconds, a piercing scream then escaped his throat as the creature released his grasp and dropped him to the ground. Mierisch toppled over and began wincing and writhing like an injured serpent. The creature peered down over him, his lips spreading into a terrible grin.

At the sound of the screams, Bexler and Wormer peered back over the sandbank and watched in horror at the events unfolding, their presence yet unnoticed. As Mierisch lay screaming uncontrollably in the sand, Hanoch turned to run. No sooner had he made three steps than the creature hurled a sharp blade in his direction. The blade planted with a striking force in the middle of the twin's back. He fell to his knees and then onto his stomach. He was gone.

Still, Mierisch continued writhing in his misery. Bexler watched as dark sores appeared all over his skin. His face began to blacken, as if boiled from the sun. He pulled up his scorched arms and ripped open his tunic, revealing the same blackening skin underneath. His whole body seemed to be smoking heavily as if thoroughly scalded. He laid there, his breath releasing in short rapid gasps. Suddenly, the Charred One reached a hand down; and catching it, Mierisch pulled himself up. His eyes were clinched tightly.

Bexler and Wormer stared down at the scene, their bodies tense with fear. Had they not witnessed the events, they wouldn't have known the new Charred One had once been Mierisch. His skin was completely black, and the same oozing bubbles arose across the surface. They glared down at the two creatures and listened as the other spoke some inaudible words to him. Suddenly, the slits of his eyes opened, revealing glazed white orbs instead of the usual dark brown iris. He was now one of them; he was a Charred One.

The two took off running toward the foothills, following the trail of the other invaders. Before they passed over the fallen Hanoch, the big one leaned down and pulled his blade from Hanoch's back. The creatures exchanged terrible grimaces and walked on, stepping on the body as they passed.

Bexler and Wormer lay motionless for some time. Upon realizing they were truly alone, Bexler let out an aggravated grunt and hobbled down to the wagon. Wormer remained in his position atop the bank, trembling uncontrollably.

"What do we do now, Bex?" he said in a rattled voice, quivering from shock.

Bexler began rummaging through items in the wagon, pulling out packs belonging to the twins. "We keep movin'," he said, appearing to be unchanged by the previous events.

Wormer sat up, wearing a look of confusion as he slid down the bank and replied, "But didn't you see what just happened?" He pointed his skinny arm in the direction of the road.

"Aye!" Bexler spit at him sharply before continuing. "And what of it?" He nodded toward Hanoch and said, "Not much we can do for 'im now, can we?"

"But—but did you know what they was gonna do to 'im?" replied Wormer.

Bexler knew to whom he was referring and resumed his work in the wagon. "Aye. I've seen it before."

"You've seen it?" Wormer paused briefly. "You knew they could do that?"

Bexler's anger began to rise and animated itself brightly across his face. "Aye! And if we stay here chattin' like li'l lasses, we've a good chance to see it again!" As he said this, he threw one pack over his shoulder and forced the other at Wormer. He pushed past him with a forceful shove, nearly knocking him to the ground.

"Where are we goin?" asked Wormer, throwing the pack across him and tightening the straps.

"After 'em. If we know where they are, we don't have ta worry about lookin' out for 'em," Bexler retorted.

Wormer gazed up ahead at the mountains, his eyes squinting through the darkness. "Yaah, okay," he replied as they too began walking along the road, careful to dodge Hanoch's body as they passed.

After a few moments, Wormer added, "How do ya suppose they do it?"

"Do what?" replied Bexler.

"Ya know—*change* 'em." His voice muffled to a slight whisper.

Bexler grimaced as he contemplated the question, then said, "They don't have to do much. The burnin's already been done inside… They just bring it out of 'em."

Wormer squinted his eyes in confusion and stared blankly ahead, wishing he hadn't asked.

The Beautiful Mystery

THADDEUS HAD NEVER BEEN SO happy to see Netheq as when he returned with the rope. Where he had found it was another issue entirely. The village had not been burned but remained in the same desolate condition as before. Everything worth having had been taken, which proved to be in their advantage as the Charred Ones marched on past the village. Whatever they were looking for was obviously not there.

Deciding they needed to keep moving, the two unlikely travellers kept near to the road. They had been walking for several hours when they heard the screams. Thaddeus's eyes grew large as he gazed in the direction of the noise. Netheq came to a sudden halt and narrowed his eyes in the darkness. He pointed his finger and nodded in the direction of an embankment a few yards ahead. Understanding his meaning, Thaddeus nodded, and they took off for their target.

It took them only a few moments to reach the top of the embankment, and upon their arrival, Thaddeus threw himself down onto the soft sand. Netheq lay upon his stomach, peering over the dunes for a proper vantage point. When it appeared they were alone, he turned over on his back and positioned his arms behind his head in a rather relaxed fashion that made Thaddeus smirk. He reclined back in a similar manner upon his pack and shut his eyes. Within a moment, he was asleep. The vision poured over him like a silk veil.

*****

A wave of cool water rushed over his feet and slid back down, tickling his legs. The sun shone high above and rested upon his face in warm bursts. His hair, nearly blinding in the sunlight, was a bright orb of golden locks, which covered his eyes in a mass of unkemptness. The sand rested in rough patches across his tanned skin. The air, thick with moisture, smelled of a recent rain and intermingled with the saltiness of the ocean in front of him. The sky was beautiful.

And then there she was—a woman. Her brown ringlets and crisp linen gown tossed about from the sweet gusts of the ocean breeze. The gown flowed loosely about her body, with the exception of her stomach, revealing that she was heavy with child. She smiled brightly, kicking the sand as she moved closer in his direction. His whole body felt warm from the inside out as familiar images rushed over him. As she sat next to him in the sand, she carefully lifted him into her lap and brushed aside his blonde hair, kissing his forehead.

Out of the corner of his eye, he saw two young boys sprinting fast into the water, laughing wildly as they dove amongst the waves and landed atop a burly man with blonde hair. Her laugh issued from the depths of her belly and lit up her whole face. He felt himself return a smile. Next, she clasped his hands in her own, placing them on his heart, and whispered something he couldn't make out. He strained to hear the words she whispered but to no avail.

He felt the image fading briskly from his mind, and he cringed at the idea of losing it. A cry escaped from his mouth as he lurched awake. His eyes opened to find Netheq, reclining directly across from him. The sun was now out, shining brightly overhead. In front of them was a small fire with a few pieces of what appeared to be a rabbit, roasting on spears. Netheq was flipping through something on his lap. Thaddeus blinked several times, clearing his vision; and narrowing his eyes, he saw what Netheq was holding. It was his sketchbook—the old one from Bexler.

Thaddeus shot up suddenly and reached viciously for his book. Netheq pulled it back with a sharp force, his eyes gazing warily at the boy.

"Give it back!" Thaddeus exclaimed, eyeing him nervously.

Netheq made no unsettled motion but merely resumed thumbing through the sketches across the pages. He stopped at the one of Bexler as a mutated ape and held it out for Thaddeus to see. The boy eyed it confusingly, then glanced at Netheq, who appeared to be smiling. Thaddeus relaxed his body and exhaled slowly as he sat down next to him.

"Yeah, it flatters him, don't you think?" Thaddeus said amusingly.

Netheq stared again at the picture and let out a slight chortle as he gently shook his head. He flipped to another page—this time to a more recent one of Wormer and the twins. The body of a mouse appeared to be running across the floor; its head was that of Wormer, wearing his usual twisted smile. At the top of the page were two cats with slanted eyes, eyeing the mouse hungrily with blasé expressions, which made them undoubtedly caricatures of the twins. Thaddeus was suddenly taken off guard as Netheq released a resounding laugh.

Thaddeus stared in awe of the sight and, taking advantage of the situation, flipped to another smaller sketch of a puckering Wormer holding a bouquet of flowers and leaning in to kiss Bexler. The two erupted in a bustle of roaring laughter. After they had flipped through several other images, Thaddeus looked up to see the contents of his pack dispersed in neat arrangements around the fire. Netheq had apparently laid them out to dry in the sun. His leather-bound book was open; the only two used pages were released from the binding and drying in the sunlight.

It was only then that Thaddeus realized Netheq had set up camp—an extremely nice one at that. He must have caught the rabbit and left him a share of the meat. As he looked around, examining the sight, a loud *thump* caused him to jolt suddenly. He turned back toward Netheq, who was sitting upright wearing an expression as if he'd just seen a ghost. His hands were frozen to the page; and as Thaddeus moved next to him, the image of the girl with the piercing eyes stared back at him.

Shrugging his shoulders and pursing his lips, he replied, "I don't know her. I just draw her sometimes." After seeing the confusion in Netheq's face, he continued, "I mean she's just someone I see when I dream." He reached to take the book from Netheq, who kept a tight grip around it and looked up at him with a speechless gaze. Pulling it firmly, Thaddeus stared back in confusion as Netheq released his hold on the book and stared intently at the ground. Silence again encircled their tiny camp.

After eating his share of the meat, Thaddeus began collecting his now dry belongings and loading them into his pack. He got the notion from Netheq's wandering eye that they better begin moving. The two set off in the direction of the mountain, neither sure of their next move. Thaddeus had never ventured this far east and was forced to rely on Netheq's lead. Before the event of the previous few days, he wouldn't have dared trust the strange man; however, given that he'd nearly saved his life twice at this point, Thaddeus felt coolly confident in his escort's guidance and followed alongside him.

As they continued along their route, Thaddeus couldn't help but think about his dream from the previous night. He hesitated to call it such as it had felt so real, like a memory he had kept locked away. The woman, the man in the water, the two boys, even the seashore—all felt strangely recognizable. His chest ached for the feeling to return. How he strained to hear the words she whispered to him!

He became so lost in his thoughts that he did not even notice the body lying motionless on the ground before him. If not for Netheq's sudden jolt along the road, he might have walked right passed it. Thaddeus snapped to his senses and stood frozen in the dusty path. Netheq held up his palm, motioning for him to stay put, as he inched closer to the corpse. Using his foot, he gently nudged at the body; and when it made no movement, he carefully lifted and rolled it onto its back. He recognized the face instantly; it was Hanoch. Glancing up, he stared at Thaddeus for several moments until waving him over.

Thaddeus's eyes gaped widely as he looked down into the face of one of the twins he had so often sketched. He shifted his gaze to Netheq, who wore a look of deep perplexity. Thaddeus need not ask to know what was pouring through the tattooed man's mind. He was sure they were the very questions running through his own. Had he crossed Bexler somehow, or was this the work of something much more evil? Neither option seemed preferable.

His thoughts were soon disrupted as Netheq bent down to grab hold of the body. He began dragging him to the side of the road. Thaddeus eyed him curiously and then, without another thought, raced over to assist him in the action. Thaddeus grabbed on to the legs, while Netheq held him under the arms; and the two of them carried the deceased man to the top of the embankment. It was there they noticed the wagon.

It was empty with no sign of Bexler or the remaining crew. Netheq lifted his face and pointed in the wagon's direction. There, they lifted Hanoch into the back and covered his face with a portion of his tunic. Thaddeus stepped back and observed Netheq with fascination. Pulling a flint stone and dagger from his tunic, he set to work creating a spark. After several minutes' attempt, a spark caught hold and ignited a tiny flame on the body lying in the wagon. Thaddeus observed carefully as Netheq pulled a piece of dry wood from the wagon's side and placed it atop the flame.

Together, they watched as the flame grew and soon engulfed the wagon. Thaddeus felt the heat increase against his face. He looked to Netheq, who stared somberly at the flame, his face glowing from the fiery grave. A mixture of fear and intrigue arose in Thaddeus as he gazed upon the strange man. Netheq was a man of mystery, but Thaddeus believed him to be intent on survival instead of corruption and that those tattoos were marks from a dark past he so desperately tried to conceal.

Part 5

MERRYN

The Forest Escape

THE SUN NESTLED CLOSELY TO the western ridge of the Shadowed Mountains as Merryn followed closely behind Brannick to the ridgeline. The fact that she was leaving her family during the onslaught of an attack left a feeling of guilt and despair in her stomach. She was running—the very thing she'd spent her whole life training not to do. And yet, here she was fleeing from a fight like a coward on the run. She thought of her family; she'd not said goodbye to Tarquin. What if she never saw them again? She forced down the sobs rising in her chest as she sprinted across the valley and into the forest. Brannick knew of the direction in which the invaders were coming, and soon they veered off course to travel around the impending raid.

The forest was thick with trees that during the spring and summer months obscured the forest with brilliant foliage of all shades. Now the harsh chill of winter left only skeletons of brown and gray behind. Although, the vast number of trees provided enough camouflage to make their escape nearly unnoticeable.

Brannick was to lead Merryn to the furthest boundaries of the valley, then retreat to the village. By then, the attackers will have laid siege against the villagers, and Merryn would be free from their grasp. *Safe*, she thought and winced at the word. Then what—travel to a land she didn't know and find a boy she's never met? She could hear the dialogue playing out in her mind.

Well, hello, Thaddeus. We've never met before, but I'm your sister. And we're a part of this sacred clan of guardians who are supposed to save the world. Oh, did I mention we have to find our two older brothers, whom we've also never met, and convince them we are not mad? And we must all embrace elements of ourselves in order for any of this to work. Oh… and also, I have no clue where to find them or what we are to do after that. Sound good? Great!

She exhaled deeply, releasing a muffled snicker of disbelief. It all sounded too preposterous for words. If she made it down the mountain alive, she still had to parade through the desert with only a name to guide her. Her head was nearly ready to explode and rather welcomed the disturbance of Brannick's deep whisper.

"I want you to climb," he said plainly.

Shaking her head of the thoughts, she stared back at him and answered in a torpid manner, "What?"

Their eyes met, breaking her from her stupor. "Climb," he repeated. "Can you do that?"

The realization of his words echoed in her ears; and in the near distance, she heard the rumbling—the growls and marching of the invaders. They were close.

Concern filling his eyes, Brannick placed his arms on Merryn's shoulders and shook her, forcefully saying, "Merryn, wake up! Don't you hear them coming?"

A shred of anger shot through her as she shoved off his hold. "Yes, I hear them!"

"Then can you climb?" he asked pointedly.

She glanced up at the trees surrounding them and saw several branches she could easily climb. "Yes," she replied. "But what will you do?" The branches would easily uphold her weight, but Brannick was a foot taller and significantly heavier than she. They would never last with the both of them.

"I will remain on foot and clear a path for us, but you are to follow closely behind me. When I run, you run. When I stop, you stop. Understand?" His words echoed sharply and directly, making Merryn forget to whom she was speaking. This was Brannick—quiet Brannick, the same boy who had just completed his *elites* along with her. Had he been withholding so much from them all these years, or was this a newfound sense of authority? Whatever it was, he was not the same boy she knew; he was stronger, more confident. She felt herself blush and nodded abruptly. Then, looking toward the sky, she made her ascent up the thin but sturdy tree and waited for the signal to begin her march.

Brannick watched as she made her ascent; and when she had reached a sufficient height, he called up to her. "Stay calm and keep your breathing light. Watch your footing and make no noise. Pay attention and follow my lead. Do not come down until I tell you."

"I've done this before," she replied with a tone of annoyance.

"Not like this," he snapped.

She rolled her eyes and was thankful he could not see her expression. Instead, she readied her footing, looking expectantly for the branches on the trees ahead to create an adequate path. Brannick made no noise as he floated along the forest floor. She allowed him to push on several paces ahead before following along her branch-laden path. Every so often, he came to an abrupt stop, no doubt to see if she was in fact paying attention, to which she herself halted suddenly; and the forest came to a hush. They continued in this manner for several minutes until Brannick appeared satisfied with her progress, and they marched on, their stops becoming fewer and fewer.

As they floated silently through the forest, Merryn remembered her *wielder* training. She won the second task of her *elites* doing exactly this, eluding even Tarquin's keen eye. But as much as she disliked admitting, Brannick was right in that she had never done so under such acute pressure. It had seemed merely a game to her before, and whether or not she was caught made no difference. Now, though, everything was different. If she were caught, would they kill her? Then she remembered the masked creature underneath the Historia—the smooth surface that covered its eyes. What if they *turned* her?

A twig snapped under her foot, and Brannick stopped suddenly. She closed her eyes, expecting him to send up a throng of insults, but all remained still. She regained her footing and waited for his movement, but he made none. Instead, he remained immobile amongst the wood. Suddenly, he lifted his arm and pointed a finger to their immediate left. She followed his finger and searched in the distance for any movement. Her eyes examined the array of massive trees encircled by even more skinny saplings. She watched fixedly as two squirrels chased each other across the branches and disappeared among the fallen leaves on the ground. Then, appearing subtly, she could just make out a scurry of action from the corner of her eye. Brannick shot down suddenly, his stomach to the forest floor, as several Charred Ones appeared from the brush and were followed by a horde of others. They were marching stealthily through the forest, their fearsome growls growing quiet as they neared their destination. Their stench soon engrossed the surrounding area. Merryn clenched her eyes together and breathed slowly through her nose, choking back the bile that was slowly working its way up her throat. Neither young wielder made any motion as the clan of invaders passed by them.

Merryn hated herself as she watched them march—the very creatures that sought to murder Anata, and she sat there doing nothing. Who would they kill? Who would they *turn*? If she were to return to Tlogluck, would it be the same place she left? There was no chance—not after an attack like this. The thoughts were unbearable; and she leaned back, heavy with exhaustion, against the wide trunk. As she tried to shake the images from her mind, her foot slipped off the branch. Her leg scraped against the rough timber as she regained control; and pulling herself behind the width of the trunk, she sat there panting roughly, trying to slow her breathing.

Fortunately, this did not disturb their march. They tread on, nearly one hundred of them, until the last one passed by; and the terrible odor faded in the distance. Several moments passed until she heard Brannick whisper lightly.

"Are you all right?" he asked. A tone of genuineness surged in his voice.

"I'm fine," she answered. "Sorry." Her voice quivered slightly as she asked, "Can I come down now?"

"Not yet. Let's move a bit further," he stated and, upon sensing her reluctance, added, "Just a bit further, I promise."

She inhaled deeply and tried to calm her shaking hands as she pressed on along the branches, her mind swimming with the same paralyzing images.

The Surprise

THEY CONTINUED WALKING FOR SEVERAL more minutes. The sun, which was beginning its descent into the western horizon when they entered the forest, had now faded slowly behind the mountains, leaving a dull glow in the sky. The forest was darkening steadily, and Merryn's trail of trees was becoming more difficult to map out. As if reading her thoughts, Brannick finally spoke.

"You can come down now," he said, his voice raspy from the silence.

Sighing a breath of relief, she began to descend along the thick branches, gliding effortlessly along the trunk. Despite her fatigue, she managed her way down with impressive speed; and upon reaching the middle half of the tree, Brannick's deep voice struck her to a halt.

"Wait! Stop moving!" A tinge of panic arose in his voice, as he remained motionless along the ground. Merryn thought back to their elites, during the sparring matches, where he assumed much of the same posture as now. His body was calm and immobile; his breathing remained slow and steady as he prepared for his assailants. His eyes were closed.

Merryn glanced around for any sign of an attacker, but she saw no one. Brannick's demeanor portrayed otherwise, however; and she remained still. Brannick inhaled and, tilting his head slightly to the right, suddenly lifted his sword from his sheath in one swift motion. Metal clanged against metal as his blade met another with a crashing blow. Merryn wheeled her head around at the sound of the first clash.

She now saw before her Brannick in full combat with a Charred One. Frozen, she clung tightly to the branches as she watched helplessly at the fight below. The beast was covered in the same hideous char as the one in the Historia but appeared to be slightly larger. He stood a couple of inches taller than Brannick; and along with the oozing sores, his body had deep slashes running diagonally across his back. At first glance, they appeared to be fresh; but as Merryn observed them more closely, they were crusted over along the edges but bright red in the middle, like a scab that had repeatedly been ripped off, a wound that would never heal.

She watched as they whirled around each other, exchanging blow after blow. The creature bounded back as Brannick moved in graceful torrents; his blade swiveled and arched in precise motions. *He was beautiful*, she thought.

As they continued, their weapons proceeded to clang loudly throughout the forest. She thought for sure they would alert the attention of more Charred Ones to their position, but nothing else appeared.

Suddenly, the creature lurched forward and drove his blade toward Brannick, who quickly knocked it from his line. The blade shifted and instead grazed the top corner of Brannick's shoulder. They pushed off one another, backing up in opposite directions. Brannick glanced at his arm, then again shut his eyes and inhaled. The creature shot a fearsome grin at Brannick. It was then that Merryn noticed its eyes. There were no irises or pupils but rather glowed in a glossy white, as if covered with a cloudy film.

Brannick remained motionless while the Charred One sprang forward, his growls echoing in the darkness. As it approached the young Swordwielder, Brannick extended his blade, shifting it behind him; and with his back facing the creature, he jerked to the side and rammed the blade into its abdomen. Then, all at once, recoiling the blade, he spun rapidly and landed panting on the ground. A second later, the Charred One's head fell beside its feet, its body crumpled to the forest floor in a heap of powdered ash.

Merryn exhaled swiftly as the events spun in her mind. They had lasted only a few moments, but she played them over as if a lifetime of action had just taken place. Briskly, she scurried down the tree and landed carefully on the ground, a grin widening across her face. But before she uttered a word, a thick arm wrapped around her as the stench encompassed her senses. Quickly, it spun her around, and she stared up at another much smaller Charred One with almond-shaped eyes—and, suddenly recalling Tarquin's words, shut her own.

The forest was already growing darker by the minute, but with her eyes clinched tightly, she was completely blind. She thought about her training—about the blindfold—and her total reliance on everything but her vision. Tarquin spoke always of how our sight blinds us, crippling our senses, denying us the ability to feel and see beyond what was right in front of our eyes. She never truly understood his words until now—this very moment. All along, he had been training her, preparing her, to fight against the Charred Ones, a darkness that ran amongst the light. And now she stood face to face with one.

She could hear Brannick rustling behind her, and she tried to breathe. The creature now had her by the throat and began lifting her up. She clenched her eyes tighter as her thoughts began to haze. She had to act, but her bones were weak. She felt her mind beginning to fade, but with it came a strange clarity. She no longer struggled against its grasp but remained still, immobile. She heard the rustle of leaves from behind her and the subtle cling of metal as it brushed across a piece of cloth. The smell of the burning Charred One fused with that of perspiration from a source inching its way closer to her. She heard the sound of a dagger rise through the air. Summoning her last bits of strength, she lifted her legs from underneath her weakened body and pressed firmly on the creature's chest; and kicking off abruptly, she flipped backward in the air, landing on the ground below as Brannick's dagger stuck firmly in the Charred One's forehead. There, lying before her feet was the creature, now nothing more than ash.

She stared in amazement. Brannick came hurdling toward her and, grabbing her firmly by the wrist, took off sprinting.

The Confession

THEY RAN FOR MILES IN the thick darkness of night, stopping briefly to catch their breaths before taking off once more. The forest seemed endless. Merryn had no idea as to its vastness and believed she might faint from exhaustion if they continued much further. She thought about what Anata had said, that Brannick was to take her to the borders and then she would travel alone. *Where would the borders end? How much further down the mountain and into the desert?* Her mind swam; she needed to rest. Suddenly without even realizing her words, she released a cry.

"I can't—I need to stop. Please." The words poured out in waves of broken cries. She felt her weight sink behind Brannick's pull. He released her wrist, and she fell to the ground. Gasping sobs sunk into the earth.

"We can't stop, Merryn… not until we reach the boundaries—"

Her words cut sharply through his response. "Then let me rest! Please! Just for a moment." She hid her face in her hands and allowed herself to sink amongst the leaves.

Brannick released a deep sigh of frustration and rubbed his hand across his face.

"Merryn, I know you're tired, but I've made an oath to get you to the border. Then I must get back—"

She again cut him off. "Go then! If upholding your duty is more important, then go!"

He stared back at her, narrowing his gaze, and released a slight chortle. "I can't believe how selfish you're being."

"Selfish?" She looked at him with a mixture of anger and confusion. "I am being selfish?" She paused and straightened up on the ground. "I was forced… against my will to follow you. I left my family and all I know behind… to chase after nothing—nothing! All I have is a name! I have no idea where I'm going or what I am to do when I get there!"

She paused, releasing gasping sobs, before adding, "If that's not enough, I just allowed the very creatures that want to murder my family to pass me by. I just let them go—I did nothing." Her voice was trembling. "And *you*—have the audacity to stand there and call *me* selfish!" So saying, she turned her gaze to Brannick, who stared back in a bewildered rage.

"And how else would you have me see it, Merryn? Hmm?" His voice barreled so forcefully that she leapt with shock. "Do you not see what is happening? Are you so naïve not to notice all that has been done—for *you*? For years, your *family* has gone through so much—endured so much to see to it that *you* were prepared for this moment. And now that you're here, you want to whine and complain because so much is happening to *you*." A deafening silence resounded like a gong in her ear. He continued saying, "You are an extraordinary girl, Merryn, but there is so much more at stake here than your comfort."

The surge of his last words crashed over her in penetrating sparks. She gazed back at him, her eyes wide with the hurtful truth of his words. She had been thinking of nothing more than what *she* wanted, how *she* felt. She had not stopped to consider what it might have cost Tarquin and Anata to keep her secret hidden for so long. The final moments in her dwelling with Tribune Sophia came rushing back to her. The way the tribune eyed her suspiciously and cast dark glares at her guardians resonated deeply in her mind. At what lengths did they go to ensure this secret?

She considered her first moments in Tlogluck—how it must have seemed for Anata to return home with a child who looked nothing like either her or her husband—the glares she must have endured. And Tarquin—she imagined him risking his position as tribune to ensure she had proper protection. How he carefully structured her training to revolve around a fight with a Charred One.

She must have been silent for some time, for Brannick moved closer to her and placed his hands upon her face, lifting her gaze to meet his. His dark eyes peered deeply into her own as he spoke softly. "I only mean to make you *see*, Merryn—see that you are stronger than you believe. You must only embrace the strength within yourself, and you'll have no idea of that which you are capable."

"But how do you know?" she asked pleadingly.

"Because I see it," he said plainly. Then he added, a slight mixture of hesitation in his voice, "I've always seen it." A prolonged hush exploded in the forest.

Breaking the silence, she added abruptly, "Why have you been so angry? You've never tried to make friends with any of us, especially me."

"I wasn't meant to become friends with you, Merryn. I was meant to protect you. I didn't want anything to stand in the way of what needed to happen when the time came." He swallowed loudly. "As for the others—they are all too afraid of me." A grin spread across his face.

She gazed at him awkwardly and pleaded with her mind to say something… anything. Before thinking, she blurted out, "Why did you do what you did to Matthew and Kristoff—that day on the sparring fields?"

"What?" He gaped, confused.

"When you choked them to the ground on our first day of training… all they wanted was to know how to hold the blade, and you completely overreacted. They couldn't talk for days afterward."

"Yaah," he said, laughing. "Well, what you didn't see or *hear*, for that matter, were the snide comments they uttered before seeking my advice on that particular issue of wielding. They weren't looking for my help, Merryn. They were *taunting* me." His voice was sharp with anger; then seeing her expression, he calmly added, "I have no doubt as to your response in the given situation. Perhaps now you'll view my overreaction as merited."

She stared at him with a look of perplexity for several seconds before asking, "Why did you agree to it?" He looked confused but knew what she meant by the question, and it hung in the air as thick as smoke. She added pointedly, "Was becoming second that important to you?"

He paused for a moment and glared at her, his face relaxing into a slight smirk. "I think we both know the answer to that," he said coolly. His nostrils flared subtly, and the look on his face made Merryn feel as if he might either try to kiss her or vomit. She wasn't quite sure which was preferable.

Merryn's eyes narrowed pensively. Then her mouth broke into a smirk. The two exchanged laughs before Brannick replied, "Now… have you had enough rest, we really must continue. We're nearly to the border, but you've still a long ways to go."

"How far to the boundaries?" she asked as she rose to her feet, wiping the leaves from her cloak.

"Not far," he said. "Maybe another hour, maybe less. Regardless, you'll have sunlight by the time you make your descent from the mountain."

Her stomach lurched at the thought of climbing down the face but did relish the fact that there would be sunlight to guide her way. Once down, she'd have only to traverse the smaller peaks nearest the foothills before making for the desert. She looked to Brannick, his dark hair flowing in a mass of knots to his shoulders. The cut on his left shoulder, now caked with dried blood, peered over his ripped tunic. He caught her gaze and replied indifferently.

"It's fine, only a scratch." A smile began to stretch across his face as he pulled his hair back securely behind his head. "Are you ready?" he asked, tightening the straps of his pack.

"I think I am," she replied. She lurched forward as she took off running, this time, Brannick trailing after her.

THE BATTLE

BRANNICK AND MERRYN MADE IT to the borders just as the sun began to peer up over the eastern ridge, but because the vast forest covered their sight from behind, their path would not have light for several more minutes. As Merryn gazed over the cliff ledge, the image before her nearly took the breath from her chest. Below she observed a vast expanse of desert sands, spotted throughout with tiny mounds she thought to be villages. In the far-off distance, she thought she could make out the waters of the Sydan Sea outlining the western horizon. A map she had seen years ago, during her principles, came rushing back to her. The Shadowed Mountains stood as the eastern border with the Sydan Sea flanking to the west. The immense Desert of Yehuda lay between the two boundaries, its sands vast and fierce. To the north lay the Forest of Vihaan; it is here where the kingly realm of Ignisia, the fire city, rests. Merryn thought about the great city and what it must have been like. Were its people—*her people*—happy?

Brannick stirred from behind, dispersing the feelings arising in her chest. His face was covered in brown mud that he had spread across much of his exposed skin in preparation for the fight he knew was coming. Merryn winced at the idea that it had already begun and that countless of villagers were either dead or turned. She whispered a prayer to the Mover for protection over her small village, as Brannick moved closer to her position along the ledge.

The sun shot brightly over the tree line, issuing a glow of orange and gold from behind them. She gazed at Brannick, who looked more like a warrior preparing for battle than the boy she once knew. He walked to the edge of the cliff and stood beside her, both of them silent as they gazed across Yehuda. Soon, the fears Merryn had tried to stifle arose in her mind, and she knew this might be the last chance she had to voice them.

"Why do they turn to ash?" she asked curiously.

Brannick made no motion but remained still and confident in his typical manner. "Because that's all they are," he answered. "When someone is turned, they burn until they are nothing but char from the inside out."

Merryn's eyes were wide with horror. "Then how—how are they alive? How can anyone survive that?"

"I don't know," he replied, a tone of frustration in his voice. "I can't understand it. All I know is that they have given in to the darkness, and it consumes them."

"How does the darkness find them?" At this question, Brannick turned his head toward her, a glint of confusion in his eyes.

"It's already there, buried deep… inside here," he said, pointing to her heart. A wave of fearful understanding began to wash over her spirit, and her eyes filled with tears.

"What if I fail?" Her voice was uncharacteristically calm and steady, but her eyes betrayed the sound.

"Then we all die," Brannick said coolly, a smirk issuing across his face.

Her face contorted into a grimace as she contemplated his words; and turning to face him, her eyes bright with shock, she smacked him hard across the chest. A laugh erupted from the two of them; and for a moment, a weight lifted from her shoulders.

She then persisted earnestly, but this time, her heart was a bit lighter. "I'm serious. What if I can't find them?"

Brannick paused briefly before answering, "You will." He sighed and looked out across the desert. "If I can leave you with anything, Merryn, it's to remember who you are." His eyes narrowed as he turned to look at her. "The Mover *chose* you. Nothing else should matter. If He chose you to fail, then you fail because there's a greater purpose yet to be revealed, and He used you in the process. If He wants the realms to be destroyed, Merryn, then they will be."

Her brow wrinkled slightly, revealing her frustration with his statement, and hung her head.

He smirked subtly then continued. "But what would be the point in that?" She glanced up again to catch his eyes with her own. "I don't believe the Mover would give in so easily. No, I believe he has a much grander idea in mind." He smiled brightly and, gazing off toward the desert, continued. "What I see in you, Merryn, is what the people of the realms need to see again—the same enduring faith that there is something greater and brighter than the darkness that so easily consumes us. If the Mover chose you for anything, it's to bring back that hope to the realms. And if you believe it, He won't let you fail—and the battle's already won."

She stared back at him for what seemed an eternity. Tears were slowly falling down her cheek.

"Then we will see each other again," she stated firmly.

He pursed his lips together, his eyes glistening from the tears he held back. "Yes, we will."

Merryn leaned forward, wrapping her arms around him tightly. Brannick closed his eyes and rested his chin atop her head. They remained locked in each other's grasp until he forced himself backward, sprinting off into the forest. She watched as his dark hair disappeared from sight. The rustling trees faded in the distance, and she was alone.

*****

The village of Tlogluck nestled itself securely in the middle of the mountain valley. From a distance, it appeared to be vacant. The villagers made no motion as the sun beamed high overhead, which should have denoted a bustle of activity, yet the village remained still. From the northern corner, a cloud of smoke appeared which encircled the small village in a ring of haze.

From the southern ridge, there suddenly appeared a thick darkness stretching across the forest line. The Charred Ones filled every gap between the trees, encasing the entrance of the forest in a putrid stench. The odor poured over the valley like a penetrating wave. The haze masked the creatures' vision but did nothing to stifle the rage in their burning hearts.

In a sudden burst of growls and screams, the Charred Ones broke through the forest line and tore through the smoky cloud encircling the field between them and the village. As their ranks crossed the ground nearing the gate into Tlogluck, a dusting of ash erupted across the burnt faces of Charred Ones running behind the frontline. A wave of Swordwielders suddenly emerged from various positions throughout the field, their blades gleaming in the bright sun, then disappearing quickly amidst the haze.

Stunned Charred Ones growled fiercely and whirled about, attempting to spy their mysterious foes. Brandishing their rusted blades, they swung through the air, cutting the smoke sharply. Several met the clang of a wielder blade, which erupted in heavy brawls. Wielders spun and twisted their blades around the burning creatures. The young apprentices from Merryn's year fought boldly and wholeheartedly, gleaming with the pride of their first battle. Piercing screams rang out through the field as men and women were turned, and the air grew thick with the ash of slain Char.

As the battle for Tlogluck raged in the field surrounding the village, Earthbearer and Lorefolk men, women, and children rested atop their refuge high in the mountains. Members of the Euphony released ancient battle cries as the winds carried their graceful melodies down the mountainside.

Among their crew were the many Swordwielder principles, too young for combat, and the numerous young apprentices. The wielder woman, who was meant to accompany them, instead made her way across the village and onto the field, donning her battle garb.

Her husband, fending off an array of Charred Ones, bellowed orders for their defenses to press on.

The battle persisted well on into the night until the final blast of ash spewed into the misty air. The sky glinted with the fading stars as the dawn eased its way up the eastern horizon. The field lay still. The bodies of fallen wielders, masked in a thick layer of gray, arrayed the ground. Several attended to the wounded who were being carried into the large Gathering Hall, cleared of its tables, for treatment. Collapsed in front of the great hearth lay Tarquin, his large body covered in deep gashes from Charred blades. His head reclined in Anata's lap; she gently caressed his face, wiping from it blood, sweat, and ash.

She smiled down on him affectionately, her eyes gleaming with an undeniable sense of pride for her husband.

His eyes were laced with fatigue and pain but failed to hide the joy exuding from their depths. A subtle smile emerged on his lips as he whispered to his bride. She leaned in closely to hear his words and shut her eyes tightly.

Her response was firm and sweet. "She knows. We both do, my love. Now, rest."

The Gathering Hall was quiet but bustled with activity as the wounded were treated. Mounds of other villagers, upon hearing word of their victory, poured into the hall. Earthbearers, with the assistance of Lorefolk, busied themselves preparing food for everyone, while the Euphony provided music to soothe and calm the weary wielders.

It was this image to which Brannick returned, though he saw nothing. Crashing into the great doors of the Gathering Hall, he collapsed to his knees as the image of surrounding villagers faded to darkness.

The Face

MERRYN SLOWLY DESCENDED THE MOUNTAIN face; its rough stone was covered in sharp protrusions and hollowed notches. Her breath, slow and steady, issued from her chest with each declining step. The air around her was thin and smelled of fresh rain and dust. Her face glowed from the bright sun, making its way high overhead. She relished the heat that radiated from its powerful energy and was stirringly thankful Brannick rushed her to the border so she'd have light by which to climb. Climbing down such a steep peak in the day was no easy task, but doing so with only the light of the moon to act as guide was terrifying. The chill of the night also offered no further support for fingers, already numb from the climb.

Judging by its height, Merryn assumed she'd make it down the face before nightfall and savored the idea of the rest that awaited her once there. It was this notion that encouraged her to continue her journey, but she also couldn't help but repeat the words Brannick had told her just before he left. She tried, however, not to think of the boy with the dark hair and eyes too much, for with him brought memories and feelings of home. Images of Anata and Tarquin encompassed her thoughts, and she quickly blinked them away. She knew what she had to do, but their memory brought up only fear and pain. She had to remain focused.

Instead, she thought about sleep… and food. It was then she'd realized she had yet to look inside the pack that Anata had sent with them. As she approached a ledge that she decided would make for a good resting place, she pulled the pack carefully around her back and lifted the flap. Pulling out its contents one by one, she examined several items.

A water pouch was the first item to greet her, to which she thirstily gulped down several drops and laid it carefully aside. Anata had packed her own cloak, a tanned animal hide that would be of much use against the harsh sands of Yehuda. She pulled out a packet of dried meats and berries and then began chewing on a piece of the meat. Toward the bottom of her pack was one of Tarquin's daggers and a coil of rope.

Gazing off into the desert, she offered another prayer to the Mover for his provision and neatly placed all of the items back into her pack. She repositioned it behind her and tightened the straps before she made her final descent to the foothills.

As she expected, night fell as she came crashing down the final slope of the mountain face. Her breath released in ragged convulsions as she pulled out the pouch of water in her pack. She took several more sips before closing the pouch and popping a few of the berries in her mouth. She threw the large cloak over her back and secured it around her neck. As she returned the other items into her pack, her hand ran across something smooth. Peering into the bag, she reached down to feel for the new object. She felt the cool metal of Tarquin's blade and the coil of rope resting at the bottom. Her brow furrowed as she searched, wondering if she had missed something. Pulling back her hand, she unexpectedly felt the small coils of metal. She gripped it around her fingers and pulled it carefully to the surface.

It was a simple golden torc with an emblem she vaguely recognized covering each end. She thought briefly to where she had seen it; then remembering the dark room in the back of the Historia, she recalled the symbol on the wall that was engraved in the stone, the one that led to the secret room below. It was the same winding symbol, now lying in her hand. A sense of confusion now shot through her as she considered what this must mean. *Why had Anata left it to me*, she wondered. This must have been a symbol of Tlogluck, and perhaps she wanted her to have something from there, but why then had she never seen it before that night? Merryn shook her head frustratingly as she wrapped the cool metal around her neck.

Sitting upright, she gazed around at the desert, now much closer, staring in amazement at its vast size. Suddenly her vision began to fail, and she felt the weight of the passed days close in around her. She felt herself fall onto her back and allow the deep sleep to engross her mind. Fatigue washed over her, deadening all senses. The night passed slowly as she dreamt; and when a set of hands reached under her, she never felt herself being lifted from the soft hills.

*****

As Thaddeus and Netheq neared the desert village of Ra'haan, a sort of strange camaraderie had appeared to brew from their time together. Perhaps the death of Hanoch changed something in Netheq, revealing more of the man behind the ink. What Thaddeus felt, however, proved to be more of a change in him than anything else. For the first time, he began to experience more of what Shamra had told him; he was again opening his heart and allowing it to feel.

The two had traveled along the road for several days before reaching Ra'haan. It lay to the far east of the Yehuda Valley and marked the furthest boundary of the desert realm. Just beyond the village were the foothills of the mountains. Netheq had not mentioned what they would do when they got to the village, but Thaddeus assumed he would want to find work with another scavenger. He also hadn't mentioned to Netheq that he wouldn't be joining him if that were the case. For now, he was content traveling alongside the tattooed man and would consider his next move when the time came.

The village was quite a bit larger than the Trader town from whence they came. It had not one but several Trader tents scattered along the main route. The quality of each tent was also quite a bit nicer than what they knew. Lining the main path between the tents were booths, not quite different from the ones in Danwebe where Thaddeus assisted Shamra each day. Their owners were bustling about attempting to sell their merchandise consisting of brightly colored shawls and necklaces of stone resembling turquoise and mother-of-pearl. Other booths smelled of strange herbs and spices that made Thaddeus's nose itch. They passed by one tent where an elderly woman with thin gray hair was selling sketches of boats with massive sails and strange creatures that possessed the body of a woman with long flowing hair, but where should be two feet was a single limb which curled up at the bottom in a round ball. Thaddeus gaped disgustingly at the image and was interrupted by Netheq's sharp elbow to his ribs.

"Owww!" he cried irritably. He glared at Netheq and would have shoved him back had he not noticed the tattooed man was gesturing to the woman in front of them. She was eyeing Thaddeus suspiciously and began limping to their position.

"What's the matter, boy? Ain't ever seen the mer-people 'afore?"

Thaddeus scrunched his face in confusion, saying, "Mer-people? That… *thing* is real?" He exchanged glances of shock from the old woman to Netheq, who stared at the picture in an odd regard.

"Aye! Ain't ya ever seen one?" she asked pointedly, to which Thaddeus shook his head hesitantly.

"Well, then how do ya know they is or ain't real?" Thaddeus was about to respond to her questions when he heard a noise that made his skin crawl. He spun around briskly and peered through the wandering customers. He eyed every booth, listening for the source of the sound.

In the distance, there stood Bexler in front of one of the larger Trader tents. Beside him was Wormer, wearing an even nastier grin than before. He appeared to be holding something in his arms.

With a concerned glare, he locked eyes with Netheq, who then quickly pulled him by the arm toward the direction of the tent. Perhaps he should have discussed with Netheq his plan not to return to the scavenger life before this moment, but now he feared it was too late. Thaddeus began to fight his way free from Netheq's grasp, kicking and pleading to be released; but the man was too strong and simply pulled him closer toward them. A crowd had begun to assemble around the tent. Bexler's newest *jewel* had obviously created quite the commotion among the village, and people were crowding around to witness the transaction.

When they neared the crowd, instead of pushing to the front, Netheq pulled Thaddeus close and wrapped his tattooed face with the hood of his cloak, gesturing to Thaddeus to do the same. A look of relief ran over him as he gently nodded at Netheq, whose eyes revealed a subtle smile. He'd apologize later, he thought. They inched their way closer to the front, careful not to draw attention to their location.

"What ya mean I can't sell her?" bellowed Bexler from the entrance to the tent. "She's just asleep, is all! See, I'll show ya." He motioned to Wormer, who then released the bundle from his grasp, letting it fall from his arms to the sand below. Much to his surprise, a small person jerked up upon impact and cowered across the ground, stirring up the sand. The head and face were covered with a tan cloak, but underneath lay a small fragile-looking frame. The stranger then arose quickly to its feet and peered anxiously around. Then, throwing the hood from the face, a cascade of long brown waves fell from the head of a young girl. A muffled gasp raced across the accumulating crowd.

At the sight of the young girl, Netheq's eyes grew wide as he stumbled backward as if the wind had been knocked from him. Thaddeus, entranced by the activity occurring ahead of him, eased his way forward. The girl, glanced to her left at a man propping himself up on a tall staff. Without another thought, she grabbed for the staff and whirling around, lashed at Wormer, knocking his feet from under him. His head crashed against the ground. Bexler's face was engulfed in rage as she pointed the staff at him, ready to knock away anyone who came close. She flipped her hair backward, revealing the long blonde streak framing her face. Her piercing eyes were a fit of fury.

Thaddeus nearly fainted. It was *her*—the girl from his drawings.

From his place amongst the crowd, Thaddeus elbowed his way through the growing mass as he leaned in to get a closer look.

Suddenly, the girl began to speak; and his feet planted beneath him, as if nailed to the dusty floor. His mouth fell open, and his eyes fixed themselves in utter disbelief.

"Thaddeus," she stammered. "I'm looking for Thaddeus," she continued, this time more intensely. Her voice was shaky and ragged from sleep, but her eyes portrayed otherwise. Bexler's face faded swiftly from anger to that of a twisted grimace.

She had found him.

Part 6

SURGE

THE DARK PRINCE

RAGGED BREATHS, GROWING LOUDER WITH each pounding step, erupted in the dark stone corridor. The remaining walls of Castle Nuria surrounded the figure, casting shadowed darkness around every bend. The air was thick with smoke, and dry heat pulsed throughout the empty chambers that once housed generations of guardians. The creature pummeled its way up the main stairway, leaving behind it the putrid stink of burning flesh and ooze with each stride. At one time, ornate carvings grazed each step of the grand staircase leading into the great hall of the castle. Now the faint outlines were buried underneath years of neglect and ash.

The Charred One's snarls issued from the depths of its throat, releasing with them vicious guttural gags and snorts. Rough patches of oozing red slits covered sections of its back and arms. As it forced open the massive doors, covered in a filmy black tar, the great hall exploded with remnants of a once grand palace. A colossal window of stained glass covered the entire left wall of the room; the panes of deep blue and purple aligned with bright gold and red were coated in a layer of gray powder. Ancient tapestries hung from the walls in tattered rags. What paintings remained on the walls, their images were burnt away, leaving nothing but the golden frames, now black from the scorch. The floor of the great hall, its polished mahogany once gleaming brightly, lay in singed disrepair. The fading image of the Halvor Crest, the emblem of the Stoneclad, rested between the layers of ash atop the floor; and a fire roared mightily ablaze in the soot-covered hearth opposite the main entry. To the far right of the great hall stood the throne pedestal; three of its four chairs lay strewn across the floor in broken heaps.

The creature, exhausted from travel, hobbled to the feet of the one remaining chair. Its occupant, a figure cloaked in a carmine robe, moved not an inch but issued from the opening of its hood a penetrating voice.

"Well?" The sound pealed fearsomely throughout the great hall.

Hesitantly, the Charred One approached the figure and spoke in a raspy tone. "No, my lord. The woman was nowhere to be found." He hung his head as he spoke.

"And what of your numbers?" asked the hooded figure.

Pausing briefly before speaking, the creature kept its head low as it said, "We were outnumbered, my lord. The villagers came from the mist and—" His words were broken off abruptly.

"You mean to tell me that an entire force of you were slaughtered by a pack of mountain farmers and not one of you laid eyes on the woman?" His voice was slow and steady, almost calm, but rang with a fearsome intensity that caused the Charred One to wrench backward.

"There were many women, my lord, and they were all skilled to fight—" As it was speaking, the figure tilted its head slightly, informing the Charred One of his disappointment. "I-it appears… so, my lor… my lord." The creature's voice was now ragged with terrors.

The figure began to rise slowly from his chair; the bottom of his cloak cascaded in a heap of dark red around his feet, pulling behind him as he made his way to where the creature stood. "And you traveled all this way to tell me—what exactly?"

"My lord?" A mixture of confusion and fear shot across the face of the Charred One as the figure began pacing in front of the pedestal.

After several moments, the hooded figure seemed unaware of the creature's presence until he repeated casually, "I am merely curious as to why then you are still here? Your entire legion is gone, and you remain here? Now tell me, what gives you that right?"

"I-I thought… you would—" The figure again cut its words short.

"Ah, yes, that's it," he said, clasping his hands together in front of his chest. "You *thought*." At this phrase, he released a dark chortle before continuing. "You see, you are a creature of the dark, a Charred One of my own design. You don't *think*. You *do*." He continued pacing the floor while he spoke; then upon finishing, he turned to face the creature that was now fidgeting nervously. Another guttural gag issued from its mouth.

"Yes, my lord, I—" But its words were once again cut short, but this time not by the voice of its master.

Suddenly, the hooded figure raised his arms, his cloak falling back to reveal a pair of charred arms. They weren't like those of the Charred Ones, however, oozing and bubbling on the surface. His skin was smooth and firm but black as tar, and his veins coursed through them a golden red. With his arms lifted toward the creature, a surge of bright red fire shot through his palms and into the chest of the Charred One. Heart-wrenching screams encircled the great hall as the creature stood writhing in pain. The figure, his face still covered by the hood, pulsed as the fiery blaze shot forth from his hands and then halted abruptly. His arms dropped to his sides as he walked around the heap of ash lay piled upon the floor. As he made his way toward the entry, he swung open the large doors, allowing a swell of hot air to force its way into the hall. He began his descent along the staircase as a pile of dust scattered its way across the great room behind him.

His walk was slow and graceful, like a serpent gliding along a slippery path. He crossed into the large corridor, where only moments ago, the Charred One's hammering footsteps and rasping breaths echoed loudly. On the ground before him lay the remains of a chandelier of immense size, shattered to bits across the vestibule. Countless candles and shards of old wax covered the stone floor and crunched under the weight of the figure's step. As he approached the enormously grand doorway, leading to the courtyard, the gigantic wooden doors opened inward as he stepped through the entryway.

The sky was dark as if a storm hovered over the ancient city of Ignisia. Frightening clouds rolled heavily overhead, blotting out the sun from its rightful place in the sky. The air held the same dry thickness as in Castle Nuria, but the heat was much more intense. The figure crossed over the desolate courtyard to the far end and peered over the edge. Below him, where once stood the great city, lay a bottomless inferno of fire, its scorching liquid boiling in a constant rumble. Around its perimeter, thousands of Charred Ones clanged hot metals while issuing their grating growls toward each other.

Upon gazing over his pit of fire, he pulled the cloak from his head, revealing a smooth skull covered in the same dark skin. The veins swirled in rivers of golden red across his skull and over his face. His eyes, pale-white orbs, gleamed terribly out across his kingdom and beyond to the vast realms awaiting his control.

THE BARGAIN

THE CROWD QUICKLY INCREASED IN size as the events unfolded around them. From inside his tent, the Trader stepped out in front of the gathered mass, dripping with curiosity. Bexler squinted his eyes suspiciously and walked up next to him.

"On second thought, I've not a mind ta sell her," stated Bexler, his eyes green with envy. As his mouth stretched into a disgustingly wide grin, his mind whirled with the potential capital he could incur from the girl's talents.

The Trader glanced at him abruptly and replied, "What? And why not? What good is she to a scavenger?"

Bexler turned to face him. "I said I'll not be selling the girl." His smiled quickly faded and gave way to a fowl grimace. His words spit forcefully over the man, who returned a nasty scowl. He towered several inches over Bexler, but the fat little man did not withdraw his glare. He bowed up his body and arched his neck as tall as possible as he said, "Ya got a problem?"

Peering down at him, the Trader glared and, releasing a slight chuckle, relaxed his shoulders. He sent a glance in the direction of the girl. While the two men were speaking, Wormer had risen to his feet and attempted to grab the staff from her grasp. She then replied with a rapid spin of the staff and, in one swishing motion, cracked it down upon Wormer's back.

After witnessing the event, the Trader stroked his chin with his hand and responded skeptically, "And just how do you propose to get her to follow you? Hmm?"

Bexler's vile grin returned to his face as he said, "'Cause… the boy she's after… he's mine." He glared at the man, whose brow narrowed slightly. Another loud crack issued from the girl's direction, grabbing their attention; and turning sharply, she took off running. Bexler broke away from the Trader and tore through the crowd as he yelled after her.

"Oy! Dollie! I wouldn't be doin' that if I's ya." She kept up her pace, breaking through the multitude as he continued to scream after her. "I know who ya's lookin' fer… and you'll not have him without me!"

She skidded to a halt but remained with her back facing him. Seeing her come to a stop, he added with a wry smile. "Aye… I knows him… Thaddeus."

Thaddeus gulped loudly from his position amongst the crowd as he turned to Netheq, who made no motion. He merely narrowed his eyes and kept them on Bexler. Without another thought, Thaddeus burst through the throng of people and up to the front, fixing his gaze on the girl. He knew her eyes—the same fierceness, an intensity he'd drawn almost every night. As he inched closer, there was something else that grabbed his attention; something about her expression exposed a deep pain, like that of great loss or longing—one he knew all too well.

She turned about slowly to face Bexler. His smile returned broadly to his face as he returned her gaze from across the crowd, who had parted in two where she had rushed through them. Now with a wide opening in between through which she could walk, she edged her way closer.

"What do you mean he's *yours*?" she asked, her face taut with uncertainty.

Bexler released an obnoxious laugh before saying, "I mean I *raised* the lad. He's practically my own flesh and blood—taught him everything I know!"

"You lie!" Her retort was stern and sharp. And as she turned to run off, Bexler continued his speech.

"No, no, I mean it—found the boy diggin' though some trash in a village not too far from here. Wasn't no bigger than this," he said, lifting his hand just above his huge waist.

"Then where is he now," she replied, raising the staff in her hands.

"Lost him... not a week ago, I did... just before the raid. Been lookin' fer him ever since," said Bexler, wiping his eye as if he'd shed a tear.

Thaddeus rolled his eyes and fought back the fit of rage shooting through him. He pictured the fat tub bouncing back and forth upon the wagon as he fled from the Charred Ones. This same man, who days ago was ready to sell his only reminder of his life with Shamra, had just taken off without a word and left him to die. This man, who truly cared nothing for him, was now supposedly struggling against the fall of tears over his absence. Thaddeus shuffled his feet lightly and prepared to jump in between the girl and Bexler. As he pushed past a short bearded man in the crowd, Thaddeus felt a sharp pull on his pack and bounded backward swiftly. Netheq had grabbed him and pulled him to the back of the crowd. He bent down so as not to reveal his face underneath his hood and spoke softly but with a firm tone.

"No, Thaddeus. You must wait." His eyes were bright with sincerity and concern. His voice rolled over Thaddeus in smooth, gentle waves, sending calming sensations throughout his body.

"But... she's looking for me! We can't let her go with Bexler," he argued, mindless to the fact that these were the first words Netheq had spoken since that night in the well.

"Neither can we let Bexler know you are here. If you speak now, you are giving him exactly what he wants."

Thaddeus paused at these words. He knew Netheq was right. But he couldn't explain the pull she seemed to have on him. He had to know her name and why her face had been at the end of his pen for years. He clenched his eyes tightly and nodded. Netheq returned the gesture and stood upright, gazing over the crowd. The girl was nearly arm's length from Bexler, who appeared to be convincing her of something. Netheq motioned for Thaddeus to stay hidden as he moved further up through the crowd to hear their conversation.

"So if I do this"—she paused—"you'll help me find him—find Thaddeus?"

"You have my word as a gentleman," Bexler replied solemnly, placing his hand over his heart.

She nor Bexler said anything for several moments as she contemplated her options, which were slim and growing slimmer by the second. "Okay… I'll do it," she said determinedly. She lifted the staff in her hands and held it out to Bexler, who motioned for Wormer to take it. He looked reluctantly from the girl to Bexler, then swiftly jerked it from her hand. A slight smirk spread across her face.

"Right then, Dollie," Bexler said. "Follow me." Bexler walked along past the girl, closely followed by Wormer, who eyed the girl menacingly. She returned the grimace before trailing along behind them.

Netheq watched sternly as the three of them trudged away from the crowd and beyond the village perimeters. The crowd slowly began to dissipate as Netheq walked over to where Thaddeus sat propped against a tent post.

"Well," Thaddeus asked inquisitively. His face was ragged with frustration and dread.

Netheq didn't stop to discuss what he'd heard with Thaddeus; instead, he walked past him, saying sternly, "Come with me, now."

Thaddeus jumped to his feet and raced after Netheq. "Where are we going?" he asked.

"To the Swallows," he said plainly.

Thaddeus ran up beside his tattooed companion and stared perplexedly into his face. "What did you say?" he asked, his words dripping with dread.

"You heard correctly," he affirmed edgily. "She's going to fight."

THE NEW LEGION

A BRIGHT LIGHT PEERED IN THROUGH the opening of the tent. Brannick's eyes cracked open as he blinked away the blinding beam. A dull ache ran throughout the course of his body, but an intense pressure surrounded his head. Raising his hand to his skull, he felt the wrappings encircling the top half of his head and winced as he touched the source of the pain. Raising himself slowly from his bed, he lifted the soft coverings from his body and discovered more bandages around his waist. A dark red stain seeped through the wrappings on his side, and bruises appeared in purple splotches along his arms and chest.

Suddenly, the image of Merryn atop a steep cliff, her hair disheveled as usual from the wind, arose in his mind. Then he remembered the Charred Ones they'd fought in the forest—Merryn flipping through the air as his blade sailed past her and into the creature's head. He thought about the embrace they shared near the ledge before he took off—leaving her to carry out her fate. His mind then rushed to his return to Tlogluck—the emptiness of the village, his fear of defeat, and his utter relief at finding its members alive in the Gathering Hall. Though much fewer in number, the village had survived the battle, and Merryn was gone. *Where was she now?*

he thought. Wherever she was, he knew he would not help her by remaining in bed; he had to do something. Pulling the remaining coverings off his legs, he again winced as he lifted them, one by one, up and off the bed. As he attempted to stand, a sharp pain shot through his head, nearly ending his endeavor.

He glanced across the room and realized he wasn't in his own chamber. The walls were bare, except for the embroidered tapestry that covered the doorway. A small desk rested against the wall to his right, its chair positioned carefully underneath. A clean stack of clothes was arranged neatly on its seat. As he motioned for the desk, the tapestry was pulled back as Anata entered, holding a tray of dressings for his wounds. He quickly reached for the blanket from his bed and wrapped it around his waist.

Her eyes were wide with surprise as she yelled sharply, "Brannick, get back in bed! You are in no condition to be moving about."

His cheeks flushed subtly as the woman approached him. She caught his gaze as he eyed the pile of clothes on the chair and said, "Don't even think about it. It has been only a few days, and you look only slightly better now than when you arrived." As she said this, she held a mirror to his face. Brannick grimaced at his reflection; he looked horrible. His dark eyes disappeared behind pits of black and blue circles. A long gash ran the length of his face at a diagonal, cutting his lips on the top and bottom of either side. The wound he had felt earlier on his head appeared much larger than he'd anticipated due to the blood that had soaked through the bandages.

Anata observed silently as he scrutinized his appearance. After several moments, she lowered the mirror. "Satisfied?" she asked, her brow furrowed into a stubborn gaze. Brannick said nothing and lowered himself steadily onto his bed, his feet resting upon the floor. Anata sighed deeply before adding, "I need to change your dressings. Then I'll send for something to eat." He nodded glumly as she began unwrapping the bandage around his head. "I must say… you are healing remarkably well. When you returned, you were so mangled we feared it had taken too much of you."

"Where is Tarquin?" he asked pointedly.

Anata avoided his gaze and waited several seconds before answering. "He's… resting," she said calmly, but her expressionless gaze exposed her concern. Anata had always been the picture of poise, during even the most stressful of times; but now, as she carefully wrapped fresh bandages around him, Brannick could see the fear in her eyes.

"Anata," he said as he gently caught her wrist. "What are you not telling me?"

Their eyes locked; and the face of a strong woman, weakened by years of struggle, flooded to the surface. Her lips quivered slightly as gentle tears pooled around her eyes. "He was injured," she said softly. "He's alive but weak."

"Take me to him," he said, his usual firm tone returning to his voice.

She nodded, then returned to her work dressing his wounds.

*****

As he entered into the tribune's chamber, he saw Tarquin, hidden behind a mass of blankets and bandages. His face was covered in jagged cuts, still a bright red where scabs had not yet formed. His eyes were closed, but upon hearing footsteps approaching, he stirred slightly.

"Anata?" he asked in a feeble tone, uncharacteristic of the strong wielder tribune.

She appeared swiftly from behind Brannick and made her way over to her husband. Positioning herself gently upon the bed next to him, she leaned in carefully and spoke in a clear smooth voice. The traces of grief from moments ago had disappeared entirely, revealing a tone of utmost affection.

"Brannick is here, my darling. He would like to speak with you if you feel able." She gently stroked the top of his head, careful to avoid the gashes that laced his skull.

A tiny slit appeared between both of his eyes as he attempted to open them. The bruising was beginning to yellow around his lids, but the swelling made opening them a difficult task. He made no attempt at sitting up but lay motionless atop his bed. But at the mention of Brannick's name, the creases of his mouth curved, revealing a subtle smile as he said, "Ah! Where's our valiant boy? Eh, forgive me, man. You've been through too much, I hear, to be called that any longer."

Brannick restrained the smirk he felt on his lips and, instead, hobbled toward the tribune. "Tarquin, has there been any news?" he asked earnestly.

Tarquin need not ask to know to whom the young man was referring. He merely sighed, then shuddered as the pain of breathing shot through him. "No. Nothing," he said plainly. "But no news… is good news, I think. Have faith." His voice pulsed in staggered phrases.

Glancing around the room, Brannick contemplated the many questions he had of the battle. The fact that he has missed it entirely troubled him deeply, but ensuring Merryn's safety overshadowed any regret he might have felt.

Returning his gaze to his leader, he asked, "And what news of our numbers?" The question was answered with nothing but silence, exposing his fear. He added reluctantly, "How many?"

Tarquin was about to speak when Anata interrupted. "We lost many *wielders*," she said. "Several were charred, forcing our own to react appropriately. Others died of their injuries." She paused briefly before adding, "The battle has taken its toll on the whole village, but its protectors are much fewer than before."

"What will you do, Tarquin?" Brannick's question hung in the air like a thick mist, engulfing the entire room in anxiety.

Anata looked to her husband, then hung her head. Tarquin replied gravely, "I… will not be doing anything, my boy." Anata turned her gaze toward Brannick, whose eyes exposed his confusion.

"I do not understand," he said. "You will heal soon. There is no need to speak this way."

"My body may heal, Brannick, but not soon enough," he stated pointedly. "There's a war waging, and my daughter is at its core. We've no time to waste."

Brannick's heart jumped beneath his chest at the thought of Merryn. He had pleaded with Tarquin and Anata to allow him to travel alongside her; but they knew, as well as he, that his services would be needed more in Tlogluck than with Merryn, a fact that was quickly emerging into reality.

"What should I do?" he asked, his expression a mixture of apprehension.

"I've no need to tell you," said the tribune confidently. "You are ready, and you already know what you will do."

At this, Anata rose from the bed and assumed a strong stance in front of Brannick. "What are your orders, Tribune?" she asked, a sad smile spreading across her face.

Brannick felt his heart leap into his throat, but what followed it was a strange reassurance. He bowed respectfully to Tarquin. Then meeting Anata's gaze, he replied, "Assemble all tribes to the Gathering Hall. We've a necessary modification to our system."

She issued an unmistakable smile of approval before marching past him. Brannick's eyes were alight with fire.

The Meeting

Merryn followed Bexler and Wormer to the far end of the village. They walked forever. It appeared they would walk past the village boundaries and into the desert's emptiness when Bexler turned left, marching toward a dingy brown tent. Several interesting characters stood around its entrance, wearing dark grimaces caked behind layers of grime. Bexler walked past them and into the tent's opening. Wormer kept his usual distance behind, smiling amusingly at each of the men lining the tent. Merryn hesitated slightly and then, hiding her apprehension, fixed her gaze firmly in front as she pushed through the cloth-lined doorway.

Inside the tent was a dank and putrid odor that caused Merryn to recoil sharply upon entering. Piles of wooden cases lined the interior walls and up to the ceiling, playing a major role in the tent's foundation. Glass bottles of all sizes lay in heaps toward the back end, while a line of animal hide hung from a wire stretching across the width of the shelter. From the appearance of the bright red flesh exposed on multiple hides, the skins were rather fresh and created the rancid aroma filling the air.

Merryn felt her face crumple into a disgusted snarl as she observed her surroundings. Bexler stood several feet in front of her and thumped his large hands onto the tall wooden pallet, doubling as a desk, in front of him. Merryn jumped at the sound of the thud as his fists crashed back down. Suddenly, a scrawny man stuck his bald head out from behind one of the enormous hanging hides. His movements were slow and snakelike as he glided his way toward their direction. As he approached, Merryn noticed the many piercings that adorned his body. The bridge of his nose was studded with two tiny gold beads, while a large round ring dangled from his nasal septum. Perhaps the most striking feature, however, was the gold chain that hung from the ring in his nose down to the clasp in his naval. He wore a tanned vest and baggy linen pants that grew significantly larger around his ankles. Slithering behind the wooden desk, he gazed down upon Bexler with wide green eyes.

"Yesss?" he hissed with a smooth lingering sound.

Bexler issued the strange man a menacing smile as he said, "I've got a fleshy for the Swallows."

Bexler continued to speak as the sinister-looking man listened eagerly, turning his attention between Bex and Wormer, who was picking absently at a scab on his arm. Bexler caught the man's incredulous glare and shook his head.

"Eh, not him," he said annoyingly and grunted as he shoved Wormer away, revealing Merryn's delicate figure behind him. "She's the one," he added fervently.

The man said nothing but tilted his head awkwardly to the side, like a bird at the sound of a screeching noise. Merryn froze. He moved his head about for several moments as he examined the small girl. The sharp penetrating gape in his eyes made her uneasy, and she pulled her cloak tightly over her shoulder. She stood as tall as she could as the man peered over her with a look of either intrigue or suspicion; she could not tell.

Several moments passed until Bexler cleared his throat and said, "Well, come on then. Let's have the draft!"

Breaking his gaze, he turned sharply to Bexler. With a shade of annoyance in his expression, he pulled a bundle of papers from underneath the desk and slapped them down between the two of them. He then pulled an old ruffled quill, several of its feathers missing, from deep within the pocket of his trousers and rested it atop the papers. Bexler gave him an irritated scowl, then reached for the quill and made his mark.

Bouncing his gaze from Merryn to Bexler, the man said in an ominous voice, "The firssst bout beginsss at sssundown." Then turning to stare at Merryn, he added, "Ssshe'll need to report to the holding now. It will transssport her to the rig." He returned his gaze to Bexler and spoke in a threatening tone. "You… will not be allowed to accompany her any further. That isss"—he paused and dispensed a final gaze toward Merryn—"until *after* the Ssswallowsss." Bexler hawked a disgusting mass from his throat and turned his eyes back to the man. The expression on his face gave Merryn an unsettling feeling in the pit of her stomach.

What have I just agreed to, she thought nervously.

As they all turned toward the tent's exit, Wormer pushed back the rags covering the entrance and met the same men from earlier who now seemed much more interested. Merryn delivered them a brief glance and noticed another who had recently joined their ranks. His cloak covered his body; but through the slit across his face, she saw the darkly colored ink surrounding his eyes. They reminded her of Tarquin, and her stomach gave a lurch. She clinched her eyes and ran after the two men in front, unaware that the cloaked figure had also dashed away hurriedly.

*****

The holding was nothing more than a cell on wheels, clad entirely from iron and wood. There were two small windows checkered over with small square ironworks. In its doorway was a rusted metal barricade whose bars were worn with scratches. Merryn hated to imagine who had been shut in there but, far worse, why they had wanted so badly to be released. A wave of nausea rushed through her body, and her palms began to sweat. She did not want to remain behind to find out. Before they reached the holding, Merryn stooped low to the ground, dodging the grips of her captors and took off running.

Wormer's grimy fingers barely missed her cloak, and his voice cracked as he yelled after her, shoving Bexler on the arm. "*Oy, Bex! She's bailin'!*"

Bexler shifted abruptly and screamed, "You'll never make it alone, Dollie! Ya don't know what's waitin' out there!"

And I don't know what's awaiting me if I get in there either! she thought, never breaking stride.

"*Go then*!" he screamed. "It's just as well. Li'l Thaddeus couldn't hack it, neither." The tone of Bexler's voice dripped with desperation as he added, "They'll get you too. You're as lost as her!"

Merryn slowed her pace to a halt and turned gently. "What do you mean? Who's lost?" she asked suspiciously.

"My Maeve," he said. His face was dowsed in free-flowing tears that took Merryn quite off her guard.

She kept her distance, eyeing him gingerly. She had never once heard him mention this name, nor had he seemed to be the most honest of creatures. He seemed a man of duplicity, and Merryn was not about to be caught in one of his schemes.

"What are you talking about?" she asked.

"My daughter, that's who." His eyes shown with genuine remorse.

Merryn inched her way closer to Bexler. Wormer stared, scratching his head in confusion. She added in a skeptical voice, "Why is it you've never mentioned her until now?"

Bexler eyed her furiously. "Not exactly something I like to bring up!" He paused. His head was shining with moisture; and pulling a disgusting yellowed cloth from his pocket, he wiped his face and the top of his bald head before continuing. "She'd be a li'l older than you by now, I'd expect." He walked over to a bench next to another trading booth and sat down with a loud thud.

Merryn walked over to where he sat on the bench. She'd never before seen him look so defeated. "What happened to her?" she asked, her voice fading into a soft murmur. Kneeling down, she lowered her head to meet his gaze. His eyes were clenched tightly, and a single tear fell down his cheek.

"I wasn't always in this line a work," he said. "No, I used ta be a trader myself, but with the good stuff, ya know—furs and beads like these people here. I had a family—a wife and girl, Maeve. Then one night, there was a raid, and they got my wife, Kesla, and took sweet Maeve with 'em." Ain't seen 'er since."

"So why do you need me?" asked Merryn, her eyes wide with pity and wonder.

"They say that the Charred Ones sometimes make trades near the coasts, if ya have something of value—something worth tradin'." As he said this, his eyes caught Merryn's.

She gave a start as the reality of his words began to take shape. "You mean—you're going to trade me for your daughter?"

He said nothing, but his silence divulged her answer. Merryn's head churned with the information. As repulsive as Bexler was, he wasn't as bad as she made him out. He once had a family—one he was trying to get back. In a sense, they shared the same purpose. She needed him to help her find her brother. He needed her to get back his daughter.

"What if she isn't alive?" She felt the sharp impact of her words as soon as she uttered them.

Bexler looked at her feverishly and replied in a voice overcome with grief, "I have ta keep tryin'."

She knew exactly what he meant. "So… ," she said, "what do I have to do?"

He glanced at her, a hint of a smile widening across his face. "Ya win," he stated boldly. "I've seen ya fight. It'll be no match fer ya."

"It?" she asked. "What exactly am I up against?"

The faint gleam in his eyes amplified into a full beam as he glared behind her toward the direction of the open sands.

*****

The air began to grow cold as the sun made its way down the westward sky. Merryn sat huddled in the small quarters of the holding cell, the day's events whirling in a buzz of perplexity. In a few moments, someone would come to retrieve her to fight in the Swallows. Bexler hadn't told her much, but what he did was enough to make anyone sick with apprehension. Not even her wielder training had prepared her for this type of sparring.

As she sat in the dank cell, memories of her life in Tlogluck began to emerge, and she forced back the lump arising in her throat as she placed her hand gently upon her neck. Her fingers brushed across the smooth metal of Anata's necklace, and a smile formed subtly upon her face. She wondered what had come of their little village—if they had survived the attack of Charred Ones, whether Anata was safe, if she was to see any of them again. As she began to sink into her feelings, her thoughts were interrupted by a sharp, "Psssssssstttttt."

Merryn leaned toward one of the small windows of the cell and asked in a hushed voice, "Who's there?"

A boy's voice rang through the cell bars. "Um… this may be hard to take in, but—uh, my name is Thaddeus."

Silence filled the small box where Merryn sat huddled next to the tiny window. When she made no answer, Thaddeus resumed, "I-I don't know if I'm who you are looking for, but…" He paused for a moment before adding, "I think I've been looking for you… for a long time."

At this statement, Anata's final words reverberated clearly in Merryn's mind: *"Look for Thaddeus. He's waiting for you."* She felt her heart leap into her chest, and her loud, shallow breaths seemed to fill the entire cell. She inched her way toward the barred door as she said timidly, "Come to the doorway. I need to see you."

Instantly, the figure of a young boy with sandy-blond hair appeared in front of her. A mixture of awe and fear filled his large green eyes as he stared back. The intensity with which he gazed upon her made Merryn recoil slightly. He reached for something from within the pack he carried on his back, and Merryn jerked abruptly.

"What are you doing?" she asked firmly.

"Easy," he said. "I just need to show you something." Lifting a small sketchbook from his bag, he slid it between the bars for Merryn to take. "Look, please," said Thaddeus, urging her to take it from him.

Merryn looked uncertainly from Thaddeus to the book before reaching her hand down to pull it through the bars. When she leaned down, gazing up at her was an intricately sketched drawing of—herself; the likeness was unmistakable. She stared fixedly in a state of sheer incomprehension for several moments before finally speaking. "How did you do this?"

His breaths began to rise in heavy bursts as he considered how to answer. Swallowing deeply, he said, "I've dreamt of your face for nearly ten years." Soft pools of tears filled his eyes as he said, almost pleadingly, "Please… tell me who you are."

Merryn gazed at him, her expression revealing her amazement. She allowed her eyes to wander over the features of his face, searching for any similarities to her own. Everything was different—the shape of his face, his eyes, the curve of his mouth. Her brow furrowed in confusion as her eye caught a subtle glint of metal at the base of his neck. She tilted her head forward, her eyes squinting eagerly.

"What's that," she said, "around your neck?"

His hand immediately flew up to his neck as he pulled at the fabric, revealing the silver relic. Merryn's eyes widened as she probed. "Where did you get that?"

"I've had it since…" Thaddeus began but stopped short as the realization came to him. "I got it the night I first *saw* you," he said, and before he could ask why, Merryn was holding her own metal emblem in front of him. "What does it mean?" he asked.

A faint smile emerged across her face as she stared through the bars at her brother. "It means I've found you—my brother," she beamed. "Or… well, that you've found me," she added, looking around at the cell walls of her holding.

Thaddeus released a slight chuckle, his eyes whirling about in amazement. Her words rang with such assurance that he knew them to be true. In fact, he had no doubt. He followed her eyes gazing around the wagon where she was held and added abruptly, "We've got to get you out of here." He peered over his shoulder and motioned for someone who then appeared suddenly beside him. It was the same man with the tattoos she saw outside the tent earlier that day. They began shaking the bars and clanging against the metal to find a weak spot through which she could escape.

When Merryn realized what they were doing, she began to contest immediately. "No, no. What are you doing? I can't leave—not now!"

Netheq continued as if he hadn't heard her, while Thaddeus shot her a baffled glance. "What are you talking about? Don't you know where they are taking you?"

"I do," she added. "But I made a promise—"

"To Bexler," he said plainly. "You can't make promises to someone who never keeps his own."

"I don't care who he is," she added firmly. "I will not go back on my word. I can do this." A look of pleading filled her eyes.

"What did he say to you?" Thaddeus asked pointedly.

Merryn wrinkled her forehead as she said, "It doesn't matter. I'm not afraid to fight one."

"One?" His tone sharpened as he probed. "What are you fighting?"

She paused briefly before answering. "A Charred One," she added cautiously.

"What?" he screamed. "You must be insane? I can't let you—"

"I'm not asking your permission. I'll be fine. I've trained my entire life for this," she said reassuringly. "Besides, I've done it before," which was only partially true. She *had* fought a Charred One, but she hadn't been alone. Brannick had actually been the one to finish it off, but she wouldn't mention that part.

As soon as the thought crossed her mind, a loud voice came barreling from the distance. "*Hey, you there, boy! Get away from there!*" A figure began sprinting toward them. Suddenly, the cell lurched forward and began moving.

Netheq pulled him back as the wagon took off. "Wait!" Thaddeus screamed. "Wait! What is your name?"

She gazed back at him, her eyes pooling with apprehension as the wagon wheeled further away. "Merryn," she yelled out. "My name is Merryn."

THE SWALLOWS

THADDEUS'S MIND WAS RACING. HE had seen her fight, but he couldn't just let her fight a Charred One. Even if she had a weapon, the creature would tower over her, and its eyes were—

But his thought was cut short as he remembered the night he'd encountered a Charred One. It was the night everything changed. He hadn't a weapon, and he was a great deal smaller, but he watched as the creature turned to ash before his own eyes. He hadn't lifted a hand. He remembered the burning on his chest as the gold symbol seared into his skin, and turning to Netheq, he said, "We have to go—now!"

Netheq nodded solemnly and took off running. Thaddeus gazed at him confusedly, then screamed after him, "What? No! You're going the wrong way! Netheq!" But it was no use. Netheq had vanished behind the tents lining the small Trader village. Thaddeus's mind was a bustle of confusion. He had found her—the girl from his drawings; and more than that, he had discovered why he had been dreaming of her. She was his sister, whom he had just allowed Bexler to take from him. *Bexler*, he thought—the very scoundrel of a man whom he had wasted ten years following was now using his sister as a means to his nasty ways. A flash of fury pulsed through his body. He could not, *would not*, allow him to get away with this. He had to do something. He glanced around for any sight of Netheq but saw nothing. The sun was setting in the distance, and the village had nearly cleared out, perhaps on their way to the arena. He had no time to think of what he would do when he got there. He'd make it up as he could. All he knew was that he had to get to the Swallows—and fast.

He heard his feet beat heavily upon the ground, kicking up blasts of sand as he skidded across the soft terrain. His breaths were short and deep, and his heart felt as if it would burst beneath his chest. Trying to shake the dreadful thoughts consuming his mind, he pressed on in the direction of the gathering horde. But the idea of what could happen to his sister—to Merryn—fought back with even more force. The strength in his legs began to fatigue, but a stronger sensation in his chest urged him to continue. The strange impulse he felt when he sketched her face upon the paper now grew with a mysterious intensity inside his very soul. He had to get to her; he had to protect her. As he pressed forward, his breath escaping viciously, his footsteps seemed to erupt into loud blows upon the sand, increasing with every step. They grew louder and louder until he felt as if his ears would burst from the noise.

His breathing was interrupted by the sound of a loud neighing from behind. He turned and nearly fell to the ground as Netheq approached upon a massive stallion. "Give me your arm," he said, his voice strangely calm.

Thaddeus wasted not a second and reached out his arm. Immediately, Netheq scooped him up and behind him upon the horse. A mixture of relief and frustration rushed over Thaddeus as he gazed at the tattoos upon the back of Netheq's head. "Thanks," he managed to utter in between ragged breaths.

"When will you stop trying to do this on your own? I'm not trying to trick you, boy," said Netheq, his eyes fixed straight ahead.

"Old habit, I guess," he replied. It was true that Netheq had proven himself trustworthy countless times over the last days. However, Thaddeus couldn't deny the fact that Netheq had been just as responsible for his captivity as Bexler. This detail surfaced each time trouble emerged, which was quite often; and he couldn't shake the feeling that Netheq was keeping something from him—something important.

As they raced on through the desert, they passed several people who were heading for the Swallows; and as they approached a gathering crowd of spectators, what he saw behind them nearly knocked him from the horse.

The Swallows was a name for not one but all of the pits of sinking sand scattered throughout the Yehuda Desert. They were invisible to the common eye, for those who knew not to look for them, but traveling with Bexler all these years had taught Thaddeus much about the desert and all of its mysteries. It was the Swallows that restricted their scavenging to the main roads rather than taking the shortcuts through the uncharted paths. It was also the reason scavengers and travellers alike were so few in number throughout the desert. If one fell into their pits, there was no way to retrieve him, for the Swallows got their namesake by no other means. As a result, Thaddeus had never actually seen the Swallows, but what stared back at him now was the single most terrifying image of his life.

There in the sands, surrounded by an incredible large mass of people, stood what had to be the largest Swallows pit in the entire Yehuda Desert. Its breadth spanned across nearly three acres of land and sloped at an angle, creating a downward funnel that sent many a fighter to a sandy grave. In the middle hung the fighting arena, a square platform suspended from its four corners by a thick rope. These were attached to tall metal poles dug deeply into the ground around the pit and upon which several people had secured a position for the fight. How they didn't break lose and send hundreds of people plummeting to the Swallows, Thaddeus had no notion; and their bloodthirsty gazes displayed no hint of concern.

They strode closer to the boundaries, which were lined several feet from the edge with wired posts to keep spectators from toppling over. Netheq pulled on the reigns, bringing the stallion to a jolting halt, and nodded for Thaddeus to jump down.

"Go find her. I'll scour the perimeter," said Netheq as he lifted the reigns and wheeled around. The horse kicked up globs of sand at a group of spectators who hurled raging insults after him. Thaddeus wasted no time and began searching for the wagon holding Merryn. Pushing through the increasing crowd, he forced his way around the first curve of the pit. Several yards ahead, a small scuffle broke out between two onlookers and quickly grew to a larger grapple among several others. The fight forced him to widen his path to the left in order to avoid the mob. Fortunately had he not, he would have walked right past the iron-barred wagon.

A crew of gruff characters surrounded the wagon heavily on all sides, making it nearly impossible to reach the iron windows. Their serious dispositions made Thaddeus believe their transport remained inside, but he had no way to reach it. His ears suddenly resounded with the yells of the vicious mob exploding to his right, and an idea surged through his mind. He looked to the man in front of him, whose back was facing the mob; and without another thought, Thaddeus shoved the man as hard as he could. The man regained his footing and spun around, fury raging across his face toward his assailant, but Thaddeus was gone. The man immediately pulled back his right arm and sent a fearsome blow to another chap directly in front of him. The two broke into a scrap along the ground. Meanwhile, Thaddeus made his way through the crowd, using the same tactic as before. One by one, brutal brawls erupted in the small space around the carriage, eventually making its way to the guards. A man with a long dark beard burst forth from within the mob and threw himself at the guard covering the back end of the carriage. Thaddeus saw his chance and ran. He reached for an iron bar and lifted himself onto the top of the enclosure. Leaning over the edge, he gazed inside; it was empty. Suddenly, a loud gong echoed in the distance. The fight had begun.

*****

The sun had set, leaving a harsh chill in the air as two guards led Merryn toward the bridge to the platform. Dull light gradually erupted from the torches encircling the pit as each one was lit. The platform in the middle glowed with the faint torchlight, making it appear even more horrifying. Merryn had not yet seen the Charred One whom she would be fighting and fervently scoured the crowd for a glimpse of her brother. She was now, more than ever, regretting her decision to fight, but her desire to keep the promise she'd made to Bexler forced her to continue without dispute. The guards shoved her forward as she willingly took the step onto the bridge and walked across, refusing to look down at the pit below. *So this was the Swallows*, she thought. The platform gave slightly under Merryn's weight, giving her no comfort for the fight ahead. Feeling the jostle, the guard behind her hesitated before tossing a rusted blade to the ground by her side and returning to his position on the opposite end of the bridge. She leaned down to reach for the blade and examined it carefully. The point was sharp, but not like that of a wielder blade; and its hilt was worn with age and misuse. The edges were caked with rust and shades of what she knew to be dried blood. She inhaled deeply and awaited the arrival of her opponent.

Soon, another loud gong erupted as the crowd abruptly parted in two, revealing the creature on the opposite end. Merryn gaped at its size. From her position yards away, the Charred One towered over the average-sized men on the ground, meaning it would be a colossal giant from her vantage up close. Her only comfort was the iron mask that encircled its head. Its eyes were covered by the smooth metal of the mask, giving it a similar appearance to the one she saw on the creature underneath the Historia. But as it made its way across the bridge, a guard tossed a set of keys on the platform in front, inches away from Merryn's feet. She stared at them disconcertedly. The platform shifted under the Charred One's weight, sending Merryn hobbling forward. The creature grunted loudly and began walking toward her direction. She regained her footing and matched its movement backward. When it had made several steps, the creature's foot brushed against the metal keys. Then it casually bent down to retrieve them. The ease with which it moved caused Merryn to wonder how many times it had done this act. What it did next, however, sent convulsive chills up her spine.

Reaching its hands behind its back, the creature lifted the keys and jostled them around the deadlock on the back of the mask.

Merryn froze. She had been told the creature would be masked, but Bexler conveniently left out the part explaining for how long. Her breaths were heavy and ragged as the lock fell to the platform. She searched the perimeters obsessively for any sign of Thaddeus, but he was nowhere to be seen. The creature wrapped its oozing hands around the mask and lifted it from its head, tossing it off the side of the platform. Merryn slammed her eyes shut, and everything went black.

I can do this, she thought. Her mind wheeled as she strained to remember her training. She thought of Brannick—of his slow, steady breaths, as if he had been dreaming—and relaxed her shoulders. She allowed her other senses to engulf her mind, replenishing what she lacked from sight. She allowed the blade to drop slowly to her side as a wave of screams exploded from around the platform. The creature was moving forward. A burst of ragged snarls erupted from her right side as she raised her blade. The metal clashed firmly against the creature's arm, sending it backward in astonishment and pain. The crowd gasped then leaped into ferocious applause. Merryn spun around and regained her position. She could smell it clearly now, the freshly carved wound intermingling with the oozing pus. The creature arched its neck and growled furiously as it lurched forward once more. Its stench permeated the air around the young wielder, and she could almost hear its anger rising. As the burning smell elevated, Merryn bent her knees and shot forward, her blade trailing behind as it sliced at the Charred One's abdomen. A mangled scream exploded from behind as she wheeled around. She knew the creature would not take much more of this, and she would have to make her move soon. The crowd's yells faded into a dull muffle as she forced them from her mind, allowing her senses to take control. Again, the stench pervaded the air as the creature drew near.

Her breathing had slowed significantly, and her hands embraced the familiar fit of the blade. She felt in control and for the first time, paid homage to the long hours of sparring with Tarquin. As the creature made its move, Merryn lifted the blade from her side and maintained her striking balance, but this time her blade met an unmoving resistance. The Charred One grasped her blade firmly in its hand

and bent it toward the ground, its mouth twisted into a nasty snarl. Merryn shook beneath the force of its strength as it forced her arm down. Grabbing the hilt of her blade with its left hand, the creature pulled the sword from her grasp and tossed it aside. She was weaponless.

She strained to maintain her composure, keeping her breaths slow and steady and her movements precise; but fear began to creep its way upon her. She had to find another way. If she could get it close to the edges, perhaps she could send it over; but this would chance her going over with it. A waft of rotten flesh whirled around her, and she rolled forward on the platform, just as the creature sent his charred fist barreling into the mat. She had no alternative. She had to try.

She lifted herself up and regained her footing. Slowly, she began backing up, one foot at a time, until she felt the ropes along the outer edges. She waited for the creature to make its move, but nothing happened. She heard no movement, nor could she smell the creature's burning flesh. Still, she remained unmoving. She thought at first it had fallen over, but that notion was quickly dismissed at the sound of an angry grunt bellowing from across the platform. She allowed her eyes to open briefly, only to see the Charred One sprinting in her direction. Merryn tightened her grasp on the rope behind her and leaped up, kicking her feet forward. The creature grabbed her legs and heaved them over its head. He was going to throw her over the edge. Merryn released a staggered scream as her body flipped over, her heels crashing into the side of the platform. Her hands set tightly around the ropes, and her shoulders ached from the twist. For the first time, her eyes were open and gazing down into the Swallows.

A surge of fear cascaded throughout her bones. She was going to fall. Then the creature grabbed her wrists. The heat from its hands scorched her skin as it lifted her from the ropes. She wouldn't fall. She was going to be thrown. Throngs of cheers burst from her surroundings. Merryn scanned the audience, and she could just make out what sounded like her name.

"*Merrrynnn!*" Thaddeus screamed at the top of his lungs. From his position on top of the carriage, he could clearly see the fight commence on the platform. He had been screaming desperately for several minutes, trying to get her attention. By now, his voice was hoarse and his throat raw, but he couldn't stop. He stood tall upon the carriage's rooftop, waving his hands over his head like a madman. Finally, hanging over the rope, Merryn's eyes caught his in the distance.

Thaddeus, she thought; he was saying something. She squinted her eyes to make out his words.

"Your torc!" he screamed, grabbing at the thick metal around his neck. "Trust yourself!"

"My torc," she said, confusion filling her mind. "The necklace?" saying aloud, she lifted her hand in order to trace the gold symbols near her throat.

"Don't be afraid!" His voice squeaked raggedly as he released these last words.

She wasn't sure what he meant, but her time was up. The creature swung her around viciously, its hand across her throat, holding her face inches from its own. Merryn clinched her eyes and struggled to free herself from its grasp, but her kicks and screams were of no use. It wanted her to *see*—to look into its eyes. She heard Thaddeus in the background, his screams slowly fading behind the cries of the fearsome crowd. He too was losing his fight; but despite the voices drowning his shouts, he pressed on relentlessly, issuing one final roar. "Look, Merryn. Trust it! Trust who you are! Look!"

Her consciousness was quickly fading as she felt the impact of his words pervade her final thoughts. *The necklace*, she thought. Her mind raced to Tarquin and Anata and to the story of the Stoneclad. *Trust who you are*, she repeated. Instantly, her mind whirled to her vision—of the dark room, the three small children, the woman upon the bed, her final words. *Remind them who they are.* Merryn squirmed violently as the creature tightened its grasp.

Thaddeus's voice whimpered amidst the crowd. "Look," he rasped as his voice died out, and he fell to his knees.

Merryn felt herself giving into the darkness surrounding her thoughts. The Charred One issued a horrible cry from the depths of its throat. Merryn took a final breath through her nose and forced her eyes open. She met the terrifying gaze of the creature's white eyes as it starred deep into her soul, searching for any sign of darkness. Any shred of hate, any ounce of greed, any envy for something more—the creature lapped up like a hungry dog. The evil residing in the souls of humanity waited as an ember prepared to ignite.

But beyond the malice, the wanton desires of life, there stood an unbreakable force—one that outshines even the darkest of evil. It is this light that shines no brighter than the flicker of a flame but extinguishes the burning within.

With Merryn in its grasp, gazing into her eyes, the creature saw this light and felt its power. Screams of an inexpressible pain jolted from the Charred One as it released its hold on Merryn, and she fell off the side. Grabbing desperately for the ropes, she struggled to hold herself up and watched as the creature covered its eyes and stumbled backward. Seconds later, an explosion of ash covered the platform.

It was gone.

EPILOGUE

THE BEGINNING

THE CROWD WENT MUTE AS silent shock brushed across the Swallows. Merryn pulled herself over the ropes and onto the solid surface of the platform. She walked toward the center and kicked around the char that blanketed its surface, her eyes cast upon the dusty pile. Then, as a violent explosion, the crowd erupted in a convulsion of cheers. Merryn gazed across the arena in inexplicable awe.

"Merryn! Yesss!" a voice from within the crowd exploded.

She spun around to see the image of her brother, leaping and screaming victoriously atop a wooden carriage. To her right, she saw the guards replacing the bridge to carry her across; and scrambling to its position, she scurried across in a wave of elation. People all around sent shouts of jubilation her way, patting her shoulders and shaking her hands as she made her way to Thaddeus. He jumped down from his position on the carriage and raced toward her direction. Upon meeting, they disappeared into each other's embrace. His arms completely encircled her as she buried her face in the folds of his tunic.

Suddenly, they were being pulled apart, and the grisly grimaces of Bexler and Wormer met their gaze. Bexler had his arms around Merryn, with the blade of a dagger firmly upon her neck. Thaddeus broke through the pitiful restraints Wormer held around him and charged after the man he so despised, but his face met a mouthful of sand as his feet went out from under him.

"Just hold it there, *Thaddeus*," came a mocking voice. "This here is *my* jewel, and I'ma gettin' what I won," Bexler snarled, hacking a wad of filth from his throat.

"Let her go, Bexler," cried Thaddeus. "You don't know what you're doing."

Bexler grinned menacingly. "I knows exactly what I'm doin'. I'ma finally gettin' my spoils."

"It's all right. I made a promise. Just let him collect the prize money, and we can go," replied Merryn calmly.

"Go? Go?" cried Bexler, a vicious laugh erupting from the fat man's chest as he and Wormer exchanged glances of sinister delight. "Ya think you can go? After what I just seen?"

A look of confusion shot across her face, as Thaddeus glared angrily. Bexler continued, "No, Dollie. Ya's stayin' right here. And, oh, the spoils we'll make from—"

But his words were cut short by the long, sharp blades outstretched toward the scavenger's throat. Wormer made a swift motion but soon faced the tip of another blade. Netheq stood tall and fierce as he held the two blades firmly in opposite directions.

"Thaddeus, get up." Gazing at Bexler, he spoke calmly. "Release the girl, Bexler, or I will finish you as I should have long ago." His voice was sharp and penetrating, and the look on Bexler's face revealed the sincerity in his words. Thaddeus lifted himself from the sand and glared at Netheq with the utmost astonishment.

Bexler's mouth twisted into a fowl grimace. "One a' these days, ole' *Netheq*. You'll be gettin' what's yours." So saying, Bexler released his hold on the girl and shoved her to the ground. He kept his eyes fixed on Netheq as he walked backward slowly. Wormer sneered nastily as he followed closely behind and disappeared amongst the crowd.

Thaddeus leaned down to lift Merryn from off the sandy ground. Brushing herself off, she looked appreciatively at her brother, then up at Netheq, eyeing the strange man inquisitively.

Following her gaze, Thaddeus grinned slightly and added, "He's a lot to take in, I know." He issued a look of warm gratitude toward the tattooed man.

Merryn nodded. "There seems to be a lot of that lately," she replied, an astonished glare crossing her face. "*Netheq* was it?" she asked as she returned her attention to the tattooed man.

But Netheq kept his eyes on the fleeing Bexler. He then began shaking his head, slowly. "No," he said firmly. Thaddeus turned his neck abruptly and cast him a look of confusion. "That is not my name," he continued.

"No? Well, what is it, then?" Merryn asked, catching her brother's look of bewilderment.

"My name is Naol," he said, turning his eyes to Thaddeus, who watched him suspiciously. "*Netheq* is no name. It's an insult, scum on the side of a ship."

"Why would he call you that? Or rather, why let him?" she probed.

Naol maintained a distant, vacant expression as he glared toward Bexler's direction. "It's where he found me," he replied. "And it soon became what I thought of myself."

Thaddeus sighed deeply as the look of confusion faded to pity. All this time he'd been branded just like him—made to feel less than. He began to feel a sense of camaraderie with the man he thought he knew for so long, only now to realize he didn't really know him at all.

Moments of silence held strong until Merryn added calmly, "Well, *Naol*, I don't know how to thank you for your help." Her eyes were alight with hope as she continued hesitantly.

Naol said nothing but rather fixed his eyes upon the two siblings.

She continued, "But, eh—I have a feeling we will be needing more of it. We've a long way to go, and I don't exactly know the way."

Thaddeus turned to Merryn and asked pointedly, "Where are we going?"

Merryn sighed heavily before saying, "West… to the Sydan Sea. That's all I know." She gazed at Thaddeus with a curious smirk before adding, "We are going to find our brother."

"Our what?" Thaddeus recoiled heavily. "We have a brother?"

"Two, actually." She smiled and released a muffled chuckle as she stated, "It's a lot to take in."

"Who—who are they? What are their names?" Thaddeus's head was spinning with the concept. He had a sister and *two* brothers. Almost instantly, images of the dream he'd had in the desert came rushing back to him. The woman heavy with child, himself, resting upon her lap, the two boys jumping through the ocean waves. "It was real," he said with an expression of complete shock.

Merryn placed her arms across his shoulders and said, "Thad, whatever it was, I am sure it *is* real." She paused as Thaddeus scrunched his eyes, revealing his confusion. "I only wish I could tell you more."

"What do you mean?" he asked.

Merryn thought momentarily and added, "What I said before—that's all I know. We have brothers, but I don't know their names. I don't know where they are. All I know is where to begin looking." Her face was alive with optimism.

Thaddeus lifted his eyes in consideration of her words, still wearing a look of skepticism.

"Don't worry," she said assuredly. "We'll find—"

"Arlo… and Elian." Naol spoke firmly. He hadn't said a word for quite some time, then continued, saying, "Those were their names." His eyes sunk to the ground and remained fixed upon the sand.

The two siblings stared fixedly, a mixture of confused delight on their faces. Several moments passed before Merryn broke the silence.

"How could you know that?" she asked.

Thaddeus took one step backward, reaching his arm out for Merryn. "Who are you? Really?"

The strange man sighed deeply before saying, "As I said, my name is Naol. I am from the Vihaan Forests, far to the west, and I was meant to protect them—to protect you." His glance shifted from between them.

Merryn's eyes were wide with amazement. "Then… that means you are of the Stoneclad," she stated, her voice rising steadily with excitement.

"I *was*, yes." Naol responded gravely.

"Was? Are you not still?" her voice shrouded with confusion.

A tender smile peered through the dark ink upon his face as he said, "I relinquished that title when you, dear Merryn, were born to us."

A wave of understanding washed over her but halted against the weight of another question. "And what of our brothers?" she asked.

His gentle expression darkened abruptly as he said, "Your brothers are dead. I lost Arlo before we could leave the city, but Elian—I saw with my own eyes."

"Dead?" Merryn gasped.

A steady firmness encircled his voice as he spoke, saying, "We were escaping the siege on the city. Arlo fell. I could not turn back."

Tears began to fill Merryn's eyes as she listened without understanding what was said. "And Elian?" she asked.

"We made it to a ship and sailed for the southern shores, but there was a storm," he said as his voice became coarse. He added harshly, "He was taken by the sea. There was no retrieving him. I washed up days later alongside a ship making port. That's where Bexler found me." A heavy emptiness enfolded Naol's eyes, and his voice lost its intensity.

Merryn exchanged looks from Naol to Thaddeus, who remained motionless, his eyes a fit of anger. She continued, "No, no. It can't be. Anata said—"

"Anata has been wrong many times. This time makes no difference!" he said with such force that Merryn jolted backward. His words frightened her.

Thaddeus remained silent as he brewed over the newfound discovery. Merryn looked to him, her eyes filled with frustration, as she screamed at him, "Thaddeus! Say something!"

"You knew," he spit the words as if bitter to the taste. "You knew, and for *years*, you said nothing, allowing me to rot in the schemes and lies of that man's filth," he screamed, motioning toward the direction Bexler had fled. "You knew I had a family. You *knew* them, and you never said anything!" Tears began rolling down his cheeks as he spoke.

Naol showed no sign of sympathy and interjected, "I had no way to know any of you were alive. I lost your brothers. Then I found you and swore to keep you safe until—"

"Until what? Until I turned out like *them*?" he screamed. His words sent stinging surges upon Naol, who remained still, brooding anger in his eyes.

"Stop it! Stop it, both of you!" Merryn's cries forced the two men to a stunned silence. Turning to Naol, she said, "I don't care what you saw. They are alive. I must believe that. I can *feel* it somehow. Otherwise, what was the point in all of this?" She placed her hand across her chest and turned to Thaddeus. "Don't you feel it, Thad?"

An expression of anger and resentment covered his face as he said, "I don't *feel* anything."

Merryn released a disappointed sigh and replied, "Well, I do—and if I'm right, our brothers are out there somewhere, and we're going to find them, *together*." She placed her hand in Thaddeus's before lifting her gaze to Naol. "With or without your help," she continued. The man stared at her dejectedly before she added, "*But* we'd get much further *with* your help." A pleading smile stretched across her face as she released Thaddeus and motioned toward Naol. "I don't know what happened, but I see your heart… your pain. And I know you did everything you could to protect them just as you did for us today. So I'm asking you now to help us make it right."

Naol turned and glared at Thaddeus, who lowered his brow. Sighing deeply, the man responded behind a wall of ink, "You don't know what you're doing."

She stared fixedly back at him and replied, "You're right, but I have faith. And I know this is much bigger than any one of us."

Naol gazed back at her, his eyes masking a sad secret. Exhaling deeply, he stated, "I can take you as far as Ka'Realle. It's a port city and marks the southern boundaries. But I cannot promise we will make it any further. There are Charred forces stationed throughout the realm. They'll be looking for you." His eyes turned and set firmly on Thaddeus.

Merryn nodded solemnly, her breaths deepening as she glanced toward the direction of their fate. The three strangers stood side by side, their bodies weary from the fatigue of the last few days. Thaddeus tightened the straps on his pack and inhaled deeply, anger still brooding in his heart.

In a few hours, the sun would make its way from the peaks of the eastern ridge, and the footsteps of the unlikely travellers would rest upon the vast sands of Yehuda, heading west toward the Sydan Sea.

Appendix

Fire… I CAN HARDLY BREATHE. I can't see him…
The flames are growing… Fire is everywhere.
Screams… I hear him… He's calling me.

"Here I am!" *I am screaming, but the smoke smothers the cries.* "I can't see you!"

Two figures appear in the distance… The clashing of metal on metal sound as gongs amongst the roar of flames.

I begin running. The heat burns each step with a growing intensity.

A stone catches my foot… I fall… A piercing cry escapes my mouth as the heat below burns my skin.

My hands turn black. I feel the tears falling down my cheeks, leaving streaks of pale skin amid a face of soot.

Stinging… burning… my hands ache… "Father!" *I scream once more.*

He turns… The tip of a blade disappears inside his chest.

The other figure… I know his face… His eyes meet my own.

"No!" *my father screams… He forces his whole being atop the other, throwing him into the crumbling wall.*

I hear the cracking of charred wood as the broken planks and billowing smoke encircle my father's assailant.

My heart pounds violently… Father…

He stumbles toward me… falling to his knees… Blood soaks his vest…

"Guide them… ," *he says… his voice choking for air…* "Without you, they are lost…"

About the Author

Elisabeth Ballard Golson is the author of *The Ember Within*, the first book in the series entitled *The Stoneclad Chronicles*. She is a graduate of William Carey University in Hattiesburg, Mississippi, where she received her degree in English. She has taught middle and high school English in Mississippi and Tennessee. She enjoys hiking, camping, kayaking, yoga, and rock climbing. She and her husband, Tyler, live in Chattanooga, Tennessee, with their son Titus and dog Louis.